slender man

SLENDER MAN

HARPER
Voyager

Harper*Voyager*
An imprint of HarperCollins*Publishers* Ltd
1 London Bridge Street
London SE1 9GF

www.harpercollins.co.uk

First published by HarperCollins*Publishers* 2018
1

A catalogue record for this book is available from the British Library

ISBN: 978-0-00-817406-4

Printed and bound in the UK by CPI Group (UK) Ltd,
Croydon CR0 4YY

welcome

Don't take this personally, but I don't like you very much.
I don't see the point of you, I resent the time I'm being forced to spend on you, and – to be honest – I just see you as an obligation, as something that I have to put up with until I can get rid of you.

But that's not going to be for a while yet, so to hell with it.

Here we go.

— — — —

March 12th
Dear Diary...

You see, that's just stupid. Why would you address a diary like it's the grandparent you only see a couple of times a year? I get that this is risky territory under the circumstances, but it seems to me that when you start talking to inanimate objects like they're people then you've reached the point where you need to check that all your screws are fully tightened. But maybe that's just me.

Either way, let's try that again.

— — — —

March 12th
Journal entry 1

Better. Much better. When I hear the word diary, I think of a bright pink book with a felt cover and a little lock and a keyhole that lives under the pillow of some twelve-year-old girl whose heart is just **so very full** of hopes and dreams and secrets. Not a Word document on the desktop of a MacBook Pro that only exists because your therapist told you it had to.

She thinks the act of writing this will be good for me, that it will help me keep things ordered and she thinks I might surprise myself. I guess there's always a chance that she's right, but I'm really not going to be holding my breath.

It's been a long time since I surprised myself.

I have to see Dr. Casemiro once a week, on Tuesday evenings after school. My parents are making me do it. I've been having nightmares for a little while now, and my mom says I've been crying out in my sleep, although part of me thinks they just got tired of being one of the only couples they know who doesn't have at least one child in therapy. I asked them why – if they're worried about me sleeping properly – they didn't just get me referred to an actual sleep therapist, and Mom told me that she thinks – and I'll quote her now – *That it's always better to get to the root of what's going on, and that it never hurts to give yourself an emotional roadworthiness test.*

I'm still not sure what she expected me to say in response to that.

Anyway.

I asked Dr. Casemiro what she wanted me to write about, whether I was supposed to keep an actual diary where I write down everything I do each day and every place I go and everyone I talk to, and she said that she wanted it *to be an outlet for personal reflection*, so what I put in it was entirely up to me.

Which was really helpful, obviously.

It must be such a weird balancing act, being a therapist. I get that the whole point is to try and lead people to realize things about themselves, rather than just tell them what's wrong, but that relies on people being brave enough to look as hard at themselves as they do at other people, and I don't know how many people are really, actually, that brave. People want easy answers, and they want pills that make them feel better.

It must be especially weird these days, where you know that if you give a patient advice that turns out to be unhelpful, they'll almost certainly sue you. That must really sharpen your professional focus, although I wonder if it makes you reluctant to actually take a position on anything. I wonder if that's why she says "Let's explore that a little further" about fifteen times every hour.

In the end, I managed to get her to at least suggest a few things that she thought it might be helpful for me to write about: family, friends, school, how I spend my spare time. Nothing that I couldn't have guessed myself, but you take what you can get, I guess.

So fine. I'll do what she says.

You know how in movies and stories, the hero usually has some destiny that they aren't aware of? Like how Luke Skywalker is destined to be a great Jedi and lead the Rebel Alliance to victory but he doesn't know it because he's living on Tattooine, or that Frodo is destined to destroy the One Ring in Mount Doom but he thinks he's going to live his entire life in The Shire?

There's a whole academic theory about it: it's called The Hero's Journey. People who go from small lives to some great grand thing, where they become part of something bigger and more important than they could ever have imagined.

I guess it's why those stories work so well, because everyone wants to believe they're more important than they really are, that any moment now some incredible thing is going to happen that turns everything upside down and they'll breathe a massive sigh of relief because they always knew they were special, *deep down they always knew it*, and all the disappointments and bullshit and trudging through dead-end days will have been worthwhile.

Me? I'm destined to be a lawyer.

Glamorous, right? **World-changing**. I can't wait.

I explained this to Dr. Casemiro during our first session, when we were still in the getting-to-know-you part of the process, and she told me I was wrong, that I can do anything with my life that I put my mind to, but all that proved is something I already knew, that a person can be **really intelligent** and **really stupid** at the same time.

Of course I can technically do whatever I want with my life. America's still just about a free country, and I'm white and male and my parents are wealthy and I go to a good school, so I have about as many advantages as it's possible for a person to have. But my options – like everyone else's – are limited by stuff that people don't like to talk about, because it doesn't fit with the all-American ideal of a meritocracy, that the only thing standing between you and your wildest dreams is hard work and a good attitude.

Which, frankly, is an absolute crock of shit.

My dad is a lawyer. Three of my four grandparents were lawyers. It runs in the family. It's in our blood.

My mom isn't a lawyer, but that's only because she got pregnant with me and never finished law school. By the time I was born my dad was the youngest partner at his firm, and I guess neither of them ever saw the point in her going back to work. I barely see her any more than I see my dad, though: she's on the boards of about a dozen charities and non-profits, and a lot of the time it seems like she works longer hours than he does.

I don't think Dad will try to tell me what major I pick when I go to college next fall, because that doesn't really effect the path he has got laid out for his only son, a path that was set in stone when I was still swimming around in his balls. But if I suggest not going to law school after I graduate? That's going to be a **really** awkward conversation.

Think of it this way:

There are things that live at the bottom of the ocean, down where only the strongest submarines can go, the ones with windows that are six inches thick. Things that are much weirder than anything in movies or novels, things that look like the guy who designed the creature out of *Alien* took a whole bunch of acid and just went nuts on a sketchpad. The pressure at the bottom of the ocean would crush a person to death in about a nanosecond, but the creatures I'm talking about thrive on it. They're used to it, because they've never known anything else.

So. Anyway.

Dr. Casemiro likes talking about my parents. LOVES talking about them, to be honest, even though I'm still scratching my head to understand how whether or not I think my mother loves me relates to me having the occasional bad dream.

I mean, I could lie and say that they neglect me, or beat me, or that dad sexually abused me when I was little, but Dr. Casemiro has met them and I don't think there's any way she would buy it. They're just too boring to have that kind of darkness inside them, even hidden away deep down where nobody else can see it.

The – equally boring – truth is that my mom and dad are kind, decent, upstanding members of the community. They probably both work more than is totally healthy, and there are times when it doesn't really feel like they're very interested in me, but find me a teenager in America who doesn't feel like that some of the time. If you can, it'll be because you've found someone who doesn't have any parents, which is a whole different thing altogether.

Jamie always tells me that I'm lucky that my mom and dad are so busy, that they always have so much stuff going on. His dad's a lot older than mine – he retired last fall, and him and Jamie's mom decided to go full super-parent for the last couple of years before their son flies the nest. Homework at the kitchen table, both of them helping out. Parent governors at Riley, both of them going along on every college visit. His mom holding the stopwatch while he does practice SAT papers. Jamie says it feels like being smothered.

Calling Jamie my best friend seems a little bit pre-pubescent girl, and calling him my bro would mean I was the kind of douchebag who actually uses the word bro. I've always liked mate, which is the British word for friend, but I don't think you can pull it off out loud unless you're Jason Statham.

He's my **closest** friend. That'll do.

We don't hang out all the time, because nobody ever really does that. And there have been times where we barely saw each other for weeks, or even months. There was the time Jamie broke his ankle playing lacrosse and I got really into *World of Warcraft*. There was the period when he was dating Lucie Goldman and just wandered around every day with this big goofy grin on his face, like he was the first person in history to ever get to third base.

But most of the time, we're pretty tight. He forwards me every dumb thing he finds on the internet, and I text him the movies he should have seen but hasn't, and we swap comics, and records, and we gossip about things that happened at school, sometimes barely minutes earlier. Because things happening aren't enough: the important part is hyper-analysing them afterwards. Obviously.

I do a lot of the same things with Lauren too, although hardly anyone knows that. She's probably my <u>oldest</u> friend, although it's not the same as it used to be, at least in public. I'm not sure most people at Riley even know that we know each other, and the weird thing is that I think both of us have sort of come to enjoy that fact. Our parents are friends, and we were super-tight until we were about eight, as stupid as that sounds now. We went to different middle schools, and when we got to Riley we lived in different worlds. But we still text all the time, and she gets to show someone every weird bit of creepypasta and the horrendous gore photos she always finds weirdly hilarious without freaking her friends out and I get to indulge my mild obsession with *Riverdale* without Jamie wondering if I've lost my mind.

It works, is what I'm saying. At school, we barely acknowledge each other. And that's OK. Because – and I'm not being hyperbolic here – Riley is a judgemental cesspit. And that's putting it mildly. It's mostly the same drama that happens in every school, the who-fucked-who, who-said-what, who-did-what stuff that seems so unbelievably important for about five minutes. Although Riley being Riley, there are times when the shit hits the fan from a slightly different direction.

There was the time one of the girls in my class had to go to the emergency room and get her stomach pumped because she had been out celebrating her mom winning a Tony.

About a quarter of the class of 2010 went from being **THE OFFICIAL KINGS AND QUEENS OF THE SCHOOL** to applying for bursaries and free lunches when Bear Stearns and Lehman Brothers went under.

Last semester two kids from the class below mine disappeared after there was a coup in the Democratic Republic of Congo and their father fled to Switzerland, taking about half the country's GDP with him. One day they were there, the next they were on a plane.

So it goes. It's a cliché to say that nobody knows what the future holds, but it's also the truth.

Nobody has a fucking clue.

— — — —

Excerpt of police interview transcript.

APRIL 22ND 2018, 20TH POLICE PRECINCT STATION-HOUSE, MANHATTAN, NY

Participants:
Detective John Staglione
Detective Mia Ramirez
Jamie Reynolds
Donald McArthur (Attorney-at-Law)

DET. STAGLIONE.   OK. Everyone set?

JAMIE REYNOLDS.   Fine.

DET. RAMIREZ.   You know you're not in any trouble, Jamie. That's been made clear to you?

JAMIE REYNOLDS.   Yeah.

DET. STAGLIONE.   We get that this is difficult.

DET. RAMIREZ.   We really do.

DONALD MCARTHUR.   Could we dispense with the "we're all friends here" act?

DET. STALGIONE.   Your attorney's a cynic.

DONALD MCARTHUR.   Detectives.

DET. RAMIREZ.   Fine. No problem.

DET. STAGLIONE.   How long have you known Matthew Barker, Jamie?

JAMIE REYNOLDS.   Since second grade.

DET. RAMIREZ.   So more than ten years?

JAMIE REYNOLDS.   I guess so.

DET. STAGLIONE.   Where was that?

JAMIE REYNOLDS.   Sorry?

DET. STAGLIONE.   Where did the two of you attend second grade?

JAMIE REYNOLDS.   Don't you know that already?

DET. RAMIREZ.   Just answer the question, Jamie.

DONALD MCARTHUR.   I'm going to ask you to take a less combative tone with my client, Detective. Mister Reynolds is not under arrest, and is cooperating fully with your investigation.

DET. STAGLIONE.   Of course. Sorry about that. So can you tell us where you met Matthew Barker?

JAMIE REYNOLDS.   At Sacred Heart.

DET. RAMIREZ.   Sacred Heart Preparatory School? On West 75th?

JAMIE REYNOLDS.   So you did know. Why ask me?

DET. STAGLIONE.   We're interested in your recollection of events, Jamie. In what you can and can't remember. We're not trying to trick you.

JAMIE REYNOLDS.   I met Matt at Sacred Heart. Like I said.

DET. RAMIREZ.   OK. Do you remember what you thought of him?

16

JAMIE REYNOLDS.   What do you mean?

DET. RAMIREZ.   Your initial impression.

JAMIE REYNOLDS.   I was seven.

DET. STAGLIONE.   So that's a no?

JAMIE REYNOLDS.   We were kids. I don't remember any more than that.

DET. RAMIREZ.   Was he popular?

JAMIE REYNOLDS.   Matt?

DET. RAMIREZ.   Yes.

JAMIE REYNOLDS.   I don't know. I mean... I guess so. Yeah. People liked him.

DET. STAGLIONE.   What about later on? At Riley?

JAMIE REYNOLDS.   He was quiet. He always has been, I guess. So he wasn't exactly the most popular kid in school. He didn't play football, and he wasn't into the kind of activities that Riley kids care about.

DET. RAMIREZ.   Which activities are those?

JAMIE REYNOLDS.   Usual shit. Debate. Band. Model UN.

DET. STAGLIONE.   And Matt wasn't into any of those?

JAMIE REYNOLDS.   No.

DET. STAGLIONE.   So what was he into?

JAMIE REYNOLDS.   Usual stuff, I guess. He liked movies, liked TV, liked games. He read a lot. He wrote stuff, too, although he never let me read any of it.

DET. RAMIREZ.   What sort of stuff?

JAMIE REYNOLDS.   Stories. Comics too, I think. I know he used to draw a lot, when we were younger.

DET. STAGLIONE.   But he wasn't unpopular?

JAMIE REYNOLDS.   No.

DET. RAMIREZ.   Did he seem happy to you?

JAMIE REYNOLDS.   What does that look like?

DET. STAGLIONE.   I don't know, Jamie. You were his friend.

JAMIE REYNOLDS.   Yeah. He seemed happy enough.

*   *   *   *

March 14ᵗʰ
Journal entry 2

I went to Whole Foods with Jamie after school let out, because he read somewhere that you burn more calories drinking wheatgrass juice than there are calories in wheatgrass juice. Which is *really, obviously* bullshit, but he says he wants to lose ten pounds before the summer because apparently he's turned into the kind of person who thinks you are supposed to weigh a certain amount at a certain time of the year and I just didn't have the energy to call him out on it. He bought two litres of the stuff and all I could think about was how green his piss is going to be before he goes to bed tonight.

We walked back through the park and he was talking about how Steve Allison has been talking shit about Lauren to anyone who will listen since she dumped him while apparently texting her about a hundred times a day asking her to take him back. I didn't really say much, even though I knew more about it than he did. He knows that we're friends – or at least, that we used to be – but he doesn't know we text all the time, because I've never told him. Like I said, it's nice to have at least one secret.

Like most of the boys at Riley, Jamie is at least a little bit in love with Lauren. I sometimes think I'm the only person who could put their hand on their heart and honestly say that they're not. It's not like I blame them – she's pretty and funny and smart and popular – but that's just not how I see her. I think I've known her too long for that. And it's hard to crush on someone who sends you videos of people walking across railway crossings and getting splattered by trains.

Anyway.

She's not the hottest girl at school. Last year there was a senior at Riley called Erin whose older sister is a Victoria's Secret Angel, and she was just about the best-looking person I've ever seen in real life. It sort of hurt to look at her, if that makes any sense. The school email server almost burned down two Septembers ago when she "accidentally" sent a folder of photos of herself in about a dozen different bikinis on the beach at Cabo San Lucas to everyone in the cheerleading squad and the athletics programs. I don't think there's ever been a link that was forwarded and downloaded more quickly in the history of the internet.

Lauren isn't as pretty as Erin was. But Lauren would also never send a folder of photos of herself in swimwear to half the senior class and claim it was an accident, so she's got that going for her.

Lauren's mom doesn't work, because her dad is this insanely sought-after gynecologist. He's clearly an asshole – he's tall and handsome and loud and is one of those guys who really pride themselves on being **CHARMING** – but he's funny, if nothing else. I was talking to him once at a parent–teacher event at Riley and he told me he's the only man in the world who has seen more supermodel vaginas than Leonardo DiCaprio. Lauren looked like she was going to die from embarrassment, but I just about fell over laughing.

I actually ran into her on Central Park West this morning and we walked to school through the park together. That happens maybe once or twice a week, and it's a good start to the day. We talked and we walked and we got coffee at one of the little carts in the park and about ten minutes later we got to Riley and told each to have a good day.

It was nice, like it always is.

In all honesty, I was glad to see her this morning because I was in a shitty mood by the time I left our apartment. I told my mom over breakfast that I wanted to stop seeing Dr. Casemiro, that it was making me feel awkward and that I clearly wasn't getting anything out of it because I'd had a nightmare two nights before, but she wasn't having any of it. She loves to really lean into that parental hypocrisy of telling me I'm an adult when she wants me to take more responsibility or stop doing something she doesn't like but refuses to actually let me make anything resembling an important decision for myself. She said the same stuff she always says: that when I'm eighteen – a legal, court-authorized adult, which is an unbelievably stupid concept if you take even a second to think about it – I can do whatever I want, including refusing to see Dr. Casemiro anymore.

Until then, I basically have to eat shit and smile about it. My words, not hers.

I told her thanks very much, but I don't think I managed to fill it with as much sarcasm as I intended, because she just nodded her head and told me to have a good day.

In fairness, it actually *was* a pretty good day, but there was no way I was going to tell her that when I got home. She got the noncommittal grunt she deserved before I came in here to my room and slammed the door. Because two can play at being unreasonable, if that's the game she wants.

No problem at all.

AP Math was painfully boring, but English was OK. We're studying *Tender Is the Night* and today we were talking about the treatment of Nicole's mental illness, about how Fitzgerald lets the reader know via flashback what's actually happening although Dick Diver keeps it a secret from the other characters for as long as he can. It carries a lot more weight when you know that Nicole is really Zelda Fitzgerald and Fitzgerald is basically telling the real story of their life together in the novel. It's clever, in a sort of meta way. I hated *The Great Gatsby*, but I'm quite enjoying this one.

We had a free period after lunch, and I got a little bit of work done on the story I've been writing. It's still not working quite how I want it to, and I'm still not totally sure how to fix it, but I wrote a few paragraphs that I'm pretty pleased with, and I think I can make them better tomorrow if I get time. I would work on them tonight, but I'm about an hour's grind from levelling up my new Warlock and I think that's about all I've got the energy for right now.

I'm really tired. Not the kind of tired where you're going to feel great if you give yourself an extra hour's sleep: that kind of deep tiredness that makes it feel like your bones are made of lead, like someone has turned all your dials down to zero and locked them.

This is what Dr. Casemiro is supposed to be helping me with. She's clearly doing an awesome job, although I'll admit that actually going to sleep before one in the morning would probably not be the worst idea in the world.

But fuck it.

I know I'm my own worst enemy :)

— — — —

From the desk of
DR. JENNIFER CASEMIRO, M.D.
596 WEST 72ND STREET, NY 10021

March 15, 2018

Dear Paul and Kimberley,
Further to our call yesterday, please find below my
assessment of my first month working with Matthew. Please
be assured that I understand your concerns about what you
perceive to be a lack of visible progress – I can only attempt
to reassure you that such progress rarely occurs at the speed
you are (understandably) hoping for and, in my experience,
its absence does not signify anything more significant than
the issues of trust-building and boundary-testing that are
common to the early stages of a professional relationship
of this type.

Matthew possesses high levels of intelligence and
awareness, and has made it clear that he is unwilling to work
with me on the issues for which he was referred. Despite
that, I believe significant progress has in fact been made.

His initial statements were that he did not want to
talk to me, and that he considered my attempts to induce

him to do so to be a violation of his human rights. This grand language is not unusual, especially in teenagers of Matthew's intelligence. It is a common form of diversion, in which he avoids the issue of why he doesn't want to talk to me by expanding our conversation to a point of general absurdity, in this case the issue of human rights.

In the last week or so, Matthew's objections to working with me have changed. He no longer states that he does not want to – he has now repeatedly stated that he does not see any point in doing so. This marks a significant shift, in my experience. He has moved past a dogmatic refusal to talk to me, and has moved onto a more personal objection, i.e. that he does not believe I can help him with what he perceives to be a medical issue. This, although it may not seem so to you, is progress. It suggests a willingness to engage with our process, provided that I can convince him of its potential usefulness. This is what I have focused on during our last two sessions.

As you know, I have asked him to keep a diary. He has apparently done so – he has shown me the pages he has written, although I (obviously) cannot guarantee that he is taking it seriously – although it is clear that he resents it. We have discussed it, however, and those conversations have been illuminating.

Persistent refusal to engage requires a level of self-control that few teenagers possess, and even Matthew, who is both intelligent and unquestionably composed, is not able to neuter his speech entirely. Our conversations have revealed the frustrations and doubts that are entirely common to this period of late adolescence, the period in which most teenagers find themselves caught between the desire to be in charge of themselves and the unavoidable reality of the rules and restrictions that come with living at home.

He makes several references to his belief that you will be disappointed in him if he chooses any career other than the law, so much so that he believes you would actually prevent it by refusing to pay for college tuition in any other field. I do not know whether this is something that you have ever made explicitly clear to him, but it has become a deeply-held belief. I suggest that you discuss this with each other, and then with him.

I am also convinced that his frustration and worry are at least partly responsible for the issue for which you referred him to my practice, i.e. recurrent nightmares and sleeplessness. This is the central issue that I will continue to focus our sessions on.

I hope this sets your mind at rest. There are no reliable timetables for the work that I do, and while I know from long experience that this can be frustrating, I would ask you to allow the process to continue. I can assure you that we are making progress, even if you are currently struggling to see it.

Yours sincerely,

Jennifer Casemiro, M.D.

TRANSCRIPTS OF AUDIO RECORDED ON MATTHEW BARKER'S CELLPHONE

Recording begins: March 16, 03:24

Jesus
That was
Hold on
Let me just

OK
OK

It's 3.24 in the morning, and I know that exactly because I've been staring at my phone screen for the last ten minutes waiting for my heart to slow down. It was on the pillow when I woke up. I must have fallen asleep still with it and right now I'm really grateful for that because if it was on the bedside table where it usually is I would have been fucked. I tried to turn on my lamp a few minutes ago and I reached out and my hand disappeared and I couldn't see it anymore and I started wondering what I would do, what I would really actually really *do*, if fingers closed around my wrist and I pulled my hand back and put it under the covers and I could feel my whole body shaking like I was freezing.

So
Jesus
I need to

Recording ends: March 16, 03:26

OK.

It's 3.30 now and it feels like my head is sort of starting to clear. I just ... Jesus. Seriously. I don't know if that was the worst nightmare I've had since they started but if it wasn't then I'm just really glad I can't remember the ones that were worse.

I can still feel it. Does that make sense? Like it was an actual thing, like a physical thing that attached itself to my skin and it feels like I can't scrape it off. Like if I close my eyes I'll be back inside it.

I managed to turn the lamp on. It took literally every ounce of bravery I've got, but I feel a little bit better now.

I never used to be able to remember dreams, not the good ones or the bad ones. I sometimes had that vague feeling when I woke up that I had been dreaming, because it felt like I wasn't really as rested as I should have been for the amount of time I'd been asleep, and sometimes there were images I didn't recognize in my head, like photographs I know I didn't take, but the dreams themselves, the details, were always gone by the time my eyes opened.

For the last couple of months it hasn't been like that. At all. And this one was no different. I can remember every single bit of it.

I already know it's going to sound stupid but right now I don't give a shit. Like, at all. Because dreams always sound stupid. They don't translate properly to other people, because they come out of some place deep inside yourself and what's absolutely fucking terrifying to me probably means absolutely nothing to you, or to anyone else. But I have to get this out. I think it will be less, afterwards. Like it's diminished or something. I don't know.

There were trees everywhere. Everywhere. That's the main thing I remember. I don't know what they were, or where. Because Central Park is two blocks away I guess it would make sense to assume that was where I was, but I don't think that's right. I didn't see any paths or gardens or anything familiar. And the trees seemed older. Like they were wild, like they had just grown wherever they wanted. I was totally surrounded by them and I remember looking up and seeing the sky, and it was black. Not dark purple or dark grey or dark blue or the pale glowing yellow that always hangs over Manhattan. Proper black.

Pitch black.

I was walking. I don't think I knew where I was going, or if I did then I've forgotten. There's no logic to dreams, no narrative of A to B to C that makes sense. Or, at least, not that I've ever known. Maybe it's different for some people.

I was walking, and there were trees and the black sky and I sort of knew that I was cold, like I was just sort of aware of it, but it didn't worry me. I just walked and shivered and walked and I can't remember actually thinking about anything, or doing anything else. I just walked.

And then
I think

Jesus. Come on, for fuck's sake. Get your shit together.

Come on
Come on

Recording ends: March 16, 03:33

Recording begins: March 16, 03:35

OK
So

There was something behind me.

I just knew there was, as surely as I know my name and where I live and that if I swing my legs out of bed there's going be a floor there. It was just a fact. It was behind me, and it was getting closer.

I didn't look round, because I think I knew that it would catch me if I did. Like that was the rule, like I was fucking Odysseus or something. If I looked round, I would see it right behind me, and I didn't want to see it. I didn't want to know what it was.

But I knew I couldn't run either. If I ran, then it would definitely catch me. I knew that too, without any doubt at all, the way some things just *are*. It's like someone installs the rules of the dream into your head before it starts.

So I kept walking. I was sort of trying to go quicker, like I was going to push the no-running rule as far as I could, but nothing really happened. That's the worst thing about dreams: that there's nothing you can do. You're basically helpless.

I know people talk about realising they're in a dream while they're still having it and being able to change things and do whatever they want, but I don't buy that. I think maybe that's how they remember them, and maybe that supposed realisation was actually just part of it, like it feels like they were making choices and exercising free will afterwards, once they're awake, but I don't think that's ever actually what happens. I don't think your consciousness is engaged in dreams. I think they're like movies with you in them, where you can't actually change what's happening. You're just a passenger along for the ride.

Anyway.

I was walking and it was dark and the thing that was behind me, whatever it was, was getting closer. It didn't make any sound, it's not like I heard its footsteps speeding up or anything like that. I just knew it was getting closer. And I knew it was going to catch me. I didn't know how long it was going to take, or whether there was any way for me to stop it, like I might reach the end of the trees and be safe. It was following me and I was walking and it was getting closer and closer and I was trying to hurry and I didn't dare look around because I knew what would happen and then I decided to run because I didn't care anymore I just needed to run because I couldn't just walk through the trees and wait for it to catch me but my legs wouldn't do what they were told and I think I screamed then but I'm not really sure and then I knew – I just absolutely knew without any doubt whatsoever – that it was right behind me and that if I reached my hand out behind my head I would touch its skin and then I definitely screamed and I felt something on the back of my neck like its breath or maybe it reached out and touched me with the tips of its fingers and

Recording ends: March 16, 03:37

Recording begins: March 16, 03:42

I've been awake for exactly twenty-eight minutes. I went to get a glass of water but my hands were shaking so much that I spilt most of it on my way back from the bathroom.

So. Yeah. I think
I think

I don't know if I screamed out loud. Probably not, because I guess someone would have woken up. The apartment is all dark and on my way back from the bathroom I stopped outside my parents room and I could hear my dad snoring.

So I guess I only screamed inside my head. It was enough to wake me up, though. My heart was racing in my chest and for the first couple of seconds I couldn't breathe, just couldn't breathe at all. It was like someone had tied a belt around my chest and pulled it tight. It was dark and the scream was ringing in my head and I couldn't see anything and I honestly thought I was dying. I thought my heart had stopped and I thought I was dying and there was a thought in my head, just one thought, going over and over and over.

It got me. I was too slow, and it got me.

Jesus

I'm pretty sure that's it for sleep for me tonight. Dad's alarm will go off in about three hours and I'm not moving from this spot until then. The lights are staying on and I'm staying right where I am and I'm not moving until the sun comes up.

I'm done

Recording ends: March 16, 03:44

LAUREN

So I read it. It's good.

MATT

You thought so?

LAUREN

I mean, I'm not exactly a literary critic. But yeah. I really liked it. The first bit, the dream, was really scary.

MATT

Awesome. I know you don't scare easily :)

LAUREN

Damn right ;)

MATT

You really liked it?

LAUREN

You know I wouldn't say so if I didn't. You should show it to someone.

MATT

I did. I showed it to you :)

LAUREN

Smartass.

LAUREN

Seriously, though. Maybe Professor Trevayne?

Message   Send

MATT

Why?

LAUREN

He might like it too?

MATT

He might. Or he might tell me it's a piece of shit. Either way, what does it matter?

LAUREN

What are you talking about?

MATT

You've met my dad, right?

LAUREN

Once or twice :)

MATT

Do you know how much writers make?

LAUREN

I would guess it depends on the writer.

MATT

Now who's being a smartass?

LAUREN

You started it.

LAUREN

Why does it matter how much writers earn?

Message Send

MATT

Because me telling my dad that I don't want to be a lawyer, that I actually want to be a writer so would he mind financially supporting me for the rest of his life, is not a conversation that's likely to go well.

LAUREN

That's bullshit.

MATT

What is?

LAUREN

Even if you're right. You enjoy writing.

MATT

Was that a question?

LAUREN

Nope. I know you enjoy it. So you should want this story to be as good as it can be.

MATT

OK.

LAUREN

So show it to someone who knows what they're talking about. Like Professor Trevayne. He gives you advice, you finish the story, then the next one you write is better. I don't see the problem.

MATT

I wish I hadn't sent it to you.

Message   Send

LAUREN

Well that's just tough shit I'm afraid.

LAUREN

I'm going to bed. Two questions first.

MATT

OK.

LAUREN

One. When are you going to send me part two?

MATT

When it's ready.

LAUREN

Spoken like a true writer :)

LAUREN

Two. What's the title going to be?

Message   Send

THE DAWN ALWAYS BREAKS

by Matt Barker

He had no idea how much time had passed when he saw it.

Time seemed malleable inside the forest, to the point where it had ceased to have any meaning. The rain had stopped briefly, then started again more heavily than ever. In the brief moments when water wasn't falling from the sky, the air had cleared and felt fresh, before thickening again as the rain returned. It had felt like the first storm had passed, only for a second, stronger one to arrive within minutes. Which was impossible, of course. The storms that battered the valley were huge, vast sheets of dark clouds that blanketed the entire sky. They took hours to move across the sky, and it was unheard of for one to follow another directly.

But that was what had happened. Stephen was sure of it.

The trail was still there, rougher and more overgrown than ever, now boggy with mud and with streams running either side of it, but it was still there. Stephen had considered what he would do if – when – it ended, if he found himself faced with the impenetrable wall of undergrowth and tree trunks that ran along both sides of the trail, but had pushed the thought away. He would deal with that if and when it became necessary to do so, and there was no sense worrying about it until then.

Thunder rolled overhead, a ceaseless drumbeat that shook great quantities of water down from the trees and trembled the trail beneath his feet. He paused, feeling the crackle in the air in his teeth and the bones of his jaw, then flinched as lightning burst across the sky, lighting the entire forest blinding white. A smell of burning filled his nose, the electricity in the air lifted the hairs on his arms and the back of his neck. The thunder rolled again, and this time he braced himself, ready for the flash when it came.

The lightning struck with a noise like the end of the world. It sounded like it was close – too close – and the blaze of light was long and hurt his eyes. In the blue-white seconds before it faded, leaving dancing spots of red and yellow in front of his eyes, he saw the scale of the place he now found himself, saw the trees stretching away in every direction, tall and old and endless. And away to his left, where the trail made a gentle turn to the left, he saw something else.

For a millisecond, he thought it was a tree. It was tall, and spindly, composed of straight lines and edges.

Then it moved…

Stephen allowed reality to come slowly, to wash over him like warm water. For long, stretched-out moments the divide between sleeping and waking was a blur of dark grey, the familiar surroundings of his bedroom bleeding into the equally familiar horror of his nightmares.

They were always the same, and he had accepted that they would never leave him. Not entirely, at least: there were nights, sometimes as many as three or four in a row, when he slept as he had before the war, and he was never less than grateful for such respite. Because he always knew it was only a matter of time before the things he had done invaded his unconscious mind again, and soaked his dreams with blood.

He swung his legs out of bed, pulled on his boots, and stood up. He felt the aches in his back, the pull of his shoulders, and grimaced. He had seen his own father stretch and wince in a similar way in the mornings, but that had been because he had been an old man. Stephen was barely thirty, although he could no longer claim with a straight face that he felt his age. He felt tired, and worn out.

He felt used up.

The physical hardships of the war had been severe, but he understood instinctively that this was something deeper. He had no learning of medicines and ailments, but he felt that a malaise had settled into his bones during his time in the west. Perhaps the old men and women of the village had been right when they proclaimed that there was a price to be paid for taking a life. If so, Stephen owed the kind of debt that would give even a king pause for thought.

He slid the bolt on his door – there had been much scoffing when he had hammered the metal plates into place, but then the farmers and blacksmiths and tailors who called the village home had never hacked a foreign king's nephew's head from his neck while his limbs still twitched and his body was still warm – and stepped out of his house.

Spread out ahead of him to the east were the fields that he had worked as a boy, first for his father and then under the unfailingly critical eye of his mother. The small stone church, abandoned since the dawn of the Age of Reason, stood at the north-west corner of the largest field. For three winters now the villagers had waited for its roof to fall in, but still it held.

To the north, the valley sloped down to the river and the rich lands beyond. It would never cease to feel strange to Stephen that when he looked in these two directions, everything he could see now belonged to him. He had protested the King's decision to make him the Lord of these lands, but only once: the King appreciated humility but did not appreciate argument, especially if the topic under discussion was a gift that was – by anyone's standards – extremely generous.

Perhaps gift was the wrong word. The lands that had always been known as Wrong Side were a reward, earned a thousand times over on the battlefield in the protection of the Realm. And had they been any other parcel of lands of equal size and value, Stephen would not have protested even once. He knew what he had done, and what it was worth. It was only the men and women who lived on and worked these lands that had given him reason to be uneasy. He had grown up amongst them, a boy no better than any other, and now he was their Lord, by order of the King.

It was fair to say that there had been varied reactions to the news.

The small village square was busy, as it almost always was.

A small queue had formed in front of the well; the hard women who worked the land with a stubborn determination that was at least the equal of their husbands, waited patiently with wooden buckets in their hands. He could not hear their voices across the distance between them and him, but Stephen was extremely confident that gossip would be flowing between them as rapidly as the water being drawn from the cool rocks below.

Down by the river, he could see clothes being washed and children playing happily along the water's edge. Arthur Allen, who would turn fifteen in a month's time and was making the most of his last summer as a boy before the duties and responsibilities of adulthood made themselves known to him, was leading a group of smaller boys and girls in a circle along the riverbanks, orchestrating a game the rules of which Stephen could not even begin to fathom. There were sticks involved, and the covering of one eye with a hand, and an intricate series of loops and whirls had been scratched into the dust. It was beyond his understanding, but the children appeared to have no such problem.

Watching the game from a tree stump at the edge of the clearing was Mary Cooper. She was already fifteen, and was now usually to be found in the Cooper fields up near the edge of the forest, turning out plough-splitting rocks and dragging twisting vine-weed up by the roots. Hard work, as Stephen knew as well as anyone. The kind of work that aged you, that added lines to the face and a stoop to the back. He was sure that would eventually be Mary Cooper's fate, unless a gentleman from the castle happened to ride down into the valley and sweep her up onto his horse and take her away to be his wife.

Mary Cooper was by no means fully grown – even though he disagreed with it, Stephen was not minded to challenge the village's assumption that fifteen was the threshold between childhood and adulthood, not when there were other matters more pressing that would cause less consternation amongst his neighbors – but the beauty she would become was already extremely apparent. Mary Cooper was a good girl, kind and decent and hardworking. Her father had died when she was young, and she and her mother lived together in a small cottage at the point where their two small fields met. She was a quiet girl, although Stephen suspected there was a hard streak in her that she could draw upon when needed: she was no fool, and she did not appreciate being taken for one, although exactly that assumption is often made about girls as beautiful as Mary Cooper.

Her hair was the color of a wheat field in afternoon sun, the lines of her face soft and pleasing to the eye, the curves beneath her dress long and smooth. Stephen had noticed the village men allowing their gaze to linger on her longer than was necessary, an occurrence that was becoming regular enough that he feared the time would come when he would no longer be able to hold his tongue.

But whereas they tried – half-heartedly in some cases – to disguise their lechery, Arthur Allen looked at Mary with the open adoration of the young, his eyes wide, his mouth almost always hanging slightly open, as though he could not truly believe the vision before him. His very open infatuation was the subject of gossip around the village, and some mocking. It was mostly gentle though, for, despite all their hard edges, the men and women of Wrong Side could – mostly – still remember what it was to be young and in love.

As he led the children in their game, Stephen saw Arthur cast stolen glances in Mary Cooper's direction. She gave no indication that she noticed – her gaze remained fixed on the slowly running river – but there was the faintest curve at the corners of her mouth, the tiniest hint of something that might – with appropriate encouragement – turn into a smile, that made him think that not only did she notice Arthur looking at her, but was content for him to do so.

Stephen watched for a little while longer, savouring the quiet contentment that had settled momentarily over the village. It wouldn't last, he knew. It never did. By mid-afternoon, when the temperature rose and so did tempers, there would be arguments that needed settling, disputes that needed resolving, and the good mood that was currently filling him would be a distant memory.

But in this moment, Stephen was content. In this moment, a thought – one that was exceptionally rare – occurred to him. He considered it, and allowed it to lodge in his mind, warming him from the inside.

This is why we went to the Borderlands, and why we waded through blood to come home.

This is what we fought for.

Stephen's first instinct, as always, was to reach for his sword.

The banging was loud, and insistent, and coming from somewhere close by. His eyes flew open, and he instantly registered that it was still dark. Not the deep night – the shutters that sealed the windows were edged in deep, velvet purple rather than rendered invisible by black – but still some hours before anyone ought to be knocking on his door.

He swung his legs out of bed and picked up his sword. It never lay out of reach, even when he was asleep, and he felt the familiar sadness at how neatly the weapon's handle fit into his hand. It had been rewrapped in leather half a dozen times, but within a few days it had always taken on some essential shape that was now part of the weapon itself. His fingers fit into faint grooves, his thumb rested against a worn blister of leather. It was an extension of himself, and even now – many months since he had last swung it in anger – he felt incomplete without it in his hand.

He crossed the small room of his dwelling in his night-shirt, his bare feet padding silently across the rolled earth. Some of the village houses had floorboards, and the grand homes that surrounded the castle had intricate tiles and even marble as floors. Stephen could have afforded the same, but such things were not in his nature. He liked the hard earth beneath his feet. He had fought for this land, killed and maimed for it, and he liked to feel connected to it.

The banging came again, long and loud. Stephen paused three yards from the door, beyond the range of any spear that might be thrust through the gap between it and the wall.

"Who goes there?" he shouted.

The reply was instant. "Sarah Cooper, my Lord."

Stephen grimaced in the darkness. The title still didn't sit well with him, and he was starting to doubt whether it ever would.

"What is it?" he asked.

"It's Mary."

"Is she hurt?"

"I don't know, my Lord," said Sarah. "I can't find her."

Stephen frowned. Then he reached out, unbolted the door, and swung it open. Sarah Cooper stood outside, her shawl pulled tightly around herself. It got cold at night in Wrong Side, even in the summer. The wind blew all the way down from the mountain, welcome during the day but capable of slicing you to the bone once the sun had set.

"What do you mean?" he asked. "When did you last see her?"

Sarah shuffled her feet against the cold. "After supper," she said. "She went out for a walk before the sun went down. Said she had thinking to do. I told her not to be more than a half hour, and she promised me she wouldn't be. That was getting on for six hours ago."

Stephen looked past Sarah to the dark silhouettes of the village. The first fingers of dawn were threatening to rise above the eastern horizon, but it would not be light for another hour, at least.

"I should have come sooner," said Sarah. "I didn't like to think bad of her, though. I know the Allen boy's been coming around, and I know they go walking some when she thinks I'm sleeping. She thinks I don't know, but I know. Ain't nothing wrong with it."

"Nothing at all," said Stephen, because he knew that was what she wanted to hear. But his attention was no longer on the frightened woman standing at his door. He was thinking about the Cooper farm, and the forest that lay just beyond its borders.

Wild things lived amongst the thick tangle of trees, things that could bite and claw. The men of Wrong Side had hunted the wolves that slid silently through the darkness almost to the point of extinction, but their howls could still sometimes be heard on the stillest nights. It was rare for them to emerge from the forest and threaten a human being, but it was not unheard of. When an animal was sick, or starving, Stephen had learnt that there was little they would not do, given the right circumstances.

There were bears in the deep forest, towering brown creatures that reared up on their hind legs and blotted out the sun. There were wildcats, barely larger than dogs but with mouths full of razor-sharp teeth and claws that could disembowel. There were snakes that spat and hissed and spiders that crawled silently over your skin, their shiny abdomens swollen with poison.

And some said there were other things too, things from before the Age of Reason that waited in the deepest dark, patient and hungry. Children told tales of such things around campfires, scaring each other silly while their parents watched on disapprovingly. There were places inside the forest – Stephen had seen them with his own eyes – where the blood in your veins ran cold and the hair on your arms stood up, even though the sun was warm overhead. Old places.

Bad places.

He was getting ahead of himself, he realized. There was more than enough bad and wicked in the world without worrying about monsters and demons. People did terrible things to other people every day, for no better reason than greed, or jealousy, or a short temper. The obvious had to be dealt with first.

"My Lord?" asked Sarah Cooper.

He looked at her. "Wake Simon Hester," he said. "Tell him I said he's to ride to the castle right away and fetch the King's Master at Arms. Tell him I said to take his fastest horse."

Sarah nodded. Her face, which had been as pale as a ghost's when Stephen opened his door, now flushed with determined color. He knew, from long experience of commanding soldiers, that people usually felt better when they had something to do, a task to focus on.

"I'll go right now," she said. "What are you going to do?"

Stephen gestured at the long night-shirt he was wearing. "I'm going to put some clothes on," he said. "And then I'm going to talk to Arthur Allen."

First time showing anyone anything. (self.writing)

submitted 2 hours ago * by breakerbreaker1989

Actually, that's a lie. I showed this to a friend of mine. But she's pretty much obliged to be encouraging, so it was only a white lie. Forgive me.

This is the first part of a story I've been working on. I'm not sure whether it's a short, or a novella, or maybe even the opening of something longer. I guess it's high fantasy with a touch of grimdark (as much as I hate that word) and I would think the influences are going to be pretty clear to anyone who gives it a look – Tolkien, Sanderson, Abercrombie, King, etc.

It's called *The Dawn Always Breaks*. 3k words. And I know this is probably a forlorn hope on a reddit sub, but please try to be kind... :)

http://www.dropbox.com/kjuehma7h
8 comments share save hide give gold report

all 9 comments
sorted by **best**

[-] **creativewritinggrad** 2 points 2 hours ago
Will check this out.
perma-link embed save report give gold reply

    [-] **breakerbreaker1989** 2 points 2 hours ago
    Thanks. Hope you enjoy it.
    perma-link embed save report give gold reply

[-] **banksculturefan** 0 points 2 hours ago
Not my thing. Sorry.
perma-link embed save report give gold reply

    [-] **moviefan2.1** 3 points 1 hour ago
    I bet OP really appreciates you taking the time to tell him that.
    perma-link embed save report give gold reply

[-] **banksculturefan** 0 points 14 minutes ago

Who cares what you think?

perma-link embed save report give gold reply

[-] **roofing_contractor_indiana** 0 points 2 hours ago

Tolkien sucks.

perma-link embed save report give gold reply

[-] **mrdoloresclaiborne** 2 points 1 hour ago

Just read the first couple of paras. Liking it so far.

perma-link embed save report give gold reply

[-] **breakerbreaker1989** 0 points 1 hour ago

Thanks a lot.

perma-link embed save report give gold reply

[-] **creativewritinggrad** 4 points 28 minutes ago

OK. Have read and digested. Here are my thoughts, for you to take or leave as you please...

On the whole, I think it's got a lot of potential – I like the style (although I'm sure you already know it needs a deep polish for repetitions and the occasional clunky sentence construction) and I like the creation of atmosphere: I can see Stephen's village clearly, and the opening sequence is enough to whet my appetite.

Stephen himself is immediately intriguing – he definitely leans into the trope of the good man who has done bad things, but that isn't necessarily a problem in itself. There is scope to do a lot with him. And the world of the story feels alive without you having deluged the reader with detail – I read a lot of fantasy and there is nothing more likely to make me put a book down than fifty pages of description of geography and family trees and complex systems of government before I even know who the main character is.

My suggestions for things for you to consider are as follows (I am aware that you may already have plans for some or all of them as the story progresses, but you asked for feedback on what is there right now):

The opening is excellently atmospheric and creepy, and I'm assuming it will serve as both a dream and a flash-forward to Stephen's search for Mary Cooper. It's a device I like, although it raises a problem: unless you intend to show us more of these prophetic dream moments, having only one might appear like cheating, as though you don't have quite enough confidence to pull readers into the story without leaping ahead to an out-of-context moment of drama.

I don't know whether you intend to flashback and show us the campaign Stephen fought in the Borderlands – if you do, then I would think very carefully about structure. It can get extremely complicated if you make the decision to have a main narrative plus flashbacks and dream-sequence flashforwards. I'm not saying you shouldn't do it, just that you will need to be very careful if you do.

And that's all I have right now. If you write more, I'd be happy to read it. Sorry if that was more criticism than you wanted, but I wouldn't have bothered if I didn't think this was a story worth continuing. It's good, and I have no doubt you'll make it better.

Best of luck with it. Peace.
perma-link embed save report give gold reply

> [-] breakerbreaker1989 0 points 8 minutes ago
> Thank you. That's given me a lot to think about. I really appreciate you taking the time to read it and to give it so much thought. It's fucking cool of you.
> perma-link embed save report give gold reply

>> [-] creativewritinggrad 0 points 4 minutes ago
>> No problem at all. Keep at it.
>> perma-link embed save report give gold reply

[-] roofing_contractor_indiana 0 points 19 minutes ago
Srsly tho. Tolkien sucks fucking donkey balls.
perma-link embed save report give gold reply

[-] creativewritinggrad 4 points 3 minutes ago

Something's been eating at me for the last half an hour or so. The dream sequence (?) opening reminded me of something, and I've been trying to place it. And I think I've got it. Did you ever read any Slender Man fic?

March 16th
Journal entry 3

I can't believe Lauren didn't pick up on that.

You wouldn't really think it to look at her, and most of her friends would be absolutely shocked to hear it, but creepypasta and nosleep and all that sort of stuff is totally her thing.

I know about Slender Man. I remember when it was massive, when there were new photoshops on reddit and somethingawful pretty much every day, when loads of people were writing **really** average stories about him and arguing about what he was and what he could do. I watched *Marble Hornets*, for fuck's sake.

I don't think that's what I was thinking about when I wrote that section. To be honest, I don't even really know what the thing in the forest was going to turn out to be, I just knew there needed to be something in there that Stephen would have to confront if he wanted to get Mary Cooper back. I think that's why I left it so vague, so I would have time to think of something good by the time I actually got to that bit.

But I can see what the guy who commented is talking about. The thin, spindly shape in the dark, the missing teenage girl, something that almost seemed to be a shadow until it moved.

I'm not sure whether I should change it or not. I don't know if I'll actually ever show it to anyone else, despite Lauren getting on my case to do so, but if I do I don't want them thinking I'm writing some cheap Slender Man fanfic. Although – to be fair – if I do show it to Professor Trevayne I really don't think it's a reference he's likely to pick up on…

I mean, everything comes from somewhere else. Nobody is immune to influences, even if they don't know they're being influenced. Everyone steals cool bits from other things, and then steal even more without knowing they're doing it. But this was the first thing I'd written in a while that I was even a little bit happy with, and I don't like the thought of anyone thinking I ripped it off from some fucking online forum.

I don't know. I'll sleep on it.

I'm sure it will be clearer in the morning.

— — — —

JAMIE

Did you hear?

MATT

About what?

JAMIE

Jesus. How can you not know? Our class group has gone fucking crazy.

MATT

I quit that group. Too annoying.

JAMIE

You need to get back in. Right now. I'll invite you.

MATT

Why? What's so urgent?

JAMIE

It's Lauren.

Message   Send

Steve Allison

Holy shit. This is crazy. None of you are even going to believe this. 06:03

Amy Linares

How come you're even awake, Steve? 06:05

Steve Allison

My mom just woke me up. Lauren's missing. 06:05

Amy Linares

What??? 06:06

Elle Solomon

What do you mean missing? 06:06

Steve Allison

I don't know. She didn't come home last night or she went out in the middle of the night. The point is she's not there. 06:07

José Sanchez

She's not home? 06:07

Steve Allison

No. Her mom called mine. 06:08

Send message

Amy Linares

Why? 06:08

Steve Allison

How the fuck should I know? I guess maybe she thought Lauren was here? 06:08

Elle Solomon

But she's not? 06:08

Steve Allison

Why the fuck would I say she was missing if she was here? 06:09

Elle Solomon

Jesus. Calm down. Did you see her yesterday? 06:09

Steve Allison

Not after school. 06:09

José Sanchez

Anyone else see her? 06:10

Bruce Underwood

Lauren's missing? 06:10

Amy Linares

Read the thread, Bruce. 06:10

Send message

Laura Muller

I saw her after school. She was coming
out of Dean & Deluca.   06:11

Elle Solomon

On Madison?   06:11

Laura Muller

Yeah.   06:11

Steve Allison

What time was that?   06:11

Laura Muller

Right after school. Maybe ten
after four?   06:12

Amy Linares

Was she on her own?   06:12

Laura Muller

I think so.   06:12

Andy Lindburgh

What's with all the notifications? If I
wanted an alarm I would have set one.   06:13

Amy Linares

Lauren Bailey's missing.   06:13

Send message   ⬯

Steve Allison
Put your fucking phone on silent then. 06:13

Andy Lindburgh
What? 06:14

Elle Solomon
She should be at home but she isn't. 06:14

Andy Lindburgh
Who saw her last? 06:14

José Sanchez
That's what we're trying to work out. 06:15

Steve Allison
Everyone stop shitposting and catching each other up. Read the thread and shut up unless you've got something useful to say. 06:15

Andy Lindburgh
Eat a dick, Steve. 06:15

Elle Solomon
So nobody saw her after I did? 06:16

Steve Allison
Fuck you Andy. 06:16

Send message

Jamie Reynolds

Jesus. This is fucked up.   06:16

Rachel Kluber

I saw her about nine.   06:16

Steve Allison

Where?   06:16

Elle Solomon

Where?   06:17

José Sanchez

You saw her?   06:17

Rachel Kluber

Outside her building. She was smoking.   06:17

Steve Allison

Did she look OK?   06:18

Rachel Kluber

She looked fine to me.   06:18

Amy Linares

That was at nine? You're sure?   06:18

Rachel Kluber

Pretty sure.   06:19

Send message

José Sanchez
What time did she go missing?   06:19

Steve Allison
Her mom didn't say.   06:20

Elle Solomon
Her building has CCTV.   06:20

Steve Allison
Obviously.   06:20

Elle Solomon
So it should be easy to work out when she left.   06:21

Amy Linares
Right.   06:21

Jamie Reynolds
Who talked to her yesterday? Did she seem OK?   06:21

Brady Goodman
I sat next to her in math. She seemed fine.   06:22

Steve Allison
What did you talk to her about?   06:22

Send message

Brady Goodman

I don't know. Nothing serious. 06:22

Steve Allison

Then how do you know she was fine? 06:23

Amy Linares

Take it easy Steve. 06:23

Brady Goodman

I didn't say she was fine. I said
she seemed fine. 06:23

Steve Allison

Don't be a fucking smartass. 06:24

Rachel Kluber

OK. Steve? I get that you're worried
but this attitude isn't helping. At all. 06:24

Brady Goodman

Fuck off Steve. 06:24

Steve Allison

Sorry. 06:24

Steve Allison

To you Rachel. Not Brady. 06:25

Send message

.ıll   89% ▰▰

Andy Lindburgh

I'm not sure this is useful. Does
anyone want to get breakfast?   06:26

Elle Solomon

I can.   06:26

José Sanchez

Me too.   06:26

Rachel Kluber

I've got spin class but I can cancel it.   06:26

Andy Lindburgh

Great. Ball and Dexter? 7.45?   06:27

Steve Allison

Are you seriously making fucking
breakfast plans right now?   06:27

Amy Linares

We're all worried.   06:27

Brady Goodman

But don't worry, Steve. We can all
see that you're the most worried.   06:28

Rachel Kluber

Seriously.   06:28

Send message   🖇

Steve Allison

Fuck you all. One of your friends is
missing. Do you get that?   06:28

Andy Lindburgh

One of our friends went out and hasn't
come home yet. Let's keep this in perspective.   06:29

Brady Goodman

Right. Go fucking White Knight
somewhere else, Steve.   06:30

Elle Solomon

So... 7.45?   06:31

March 16th
Journal entry 4

Jesus fucking Christ. Steve Allison and Lauren dated for about five minutes and now he's just about ready to go on Oprah and issue a heartfelt plea for her to come home.

We don't know anything yet. We don't know what time she went out, if she was on her own, if she had a fight with her parents, if she had plans anyone knew about. Steve's just jumping on something that will make him the center of attention. Again.

I know Lauren better than he does. I know how smart she is, how capable.

There's nothing to worry about.

She'll be fine.

I'm sure of it.

She'll be fine.

— — — —

APRIL 22ND 2018, 20TH POLICE PRECINCT STATION-HOUSE, MANHATTAN, NY

Participants:
Detective John Staglione
Detective Mia Ramirez
Jamie Reynolds
Donald McArthur (Attorney-at-Law)

DET. STAGLIONE.   Do you remember the day Lauren Bailey went missing?

JAMIE REYNOLDS.   Of course I do.

DET. RAMIREZ.   How did you hear about it?

JAMIE REYNOLDS.   Everyone was talking about it.

DET. STAGLIONE.   Did someone call you?

JAMIE REYNOLDS.   No. There were messages on my phone when I woke up.

DET. RAMIREZ.   From who?

JAMIE REYNOLDS.   Everyone. It seemed like our entire class.

DET. RAMIREZ.   There was a thread?

JAMIE REYNOLDS.   Right.

DET. RAMIREZ.   On which service?

JAMIE REYNOLDS.   Service?

DET. STAGLIONE.   Which app, Jamie. Facebook? WhatsApp?

JAMIE REYNOLDS.   Oh. Yeah. There's a WhatsApp group. Most of our class is in it.

DET. STAGLIONE.   Was Matt in it?

JAMIE REYNOLDS.   He said he dropped it. I sent him an invite that morning because it was going crazy on there, but I don't know if he accepted it.

DET. RAMIREZ.   Who started the thread about Lauren?

JAMIE REYNOLDS.   I can't remember. Maybe Steve Allison?

DET. STAGLIONE.   Were they close? Steve and Lauren?

JAMIE REYNOLDS.   They dated for a while.

DET. STAGLIONE.   That's not what I asked you.

JAMIE REYNOLDS.   Jesus. I don't know. They seemed friendly enough. How am I supposed to know how close they were?

DET. RAMIREZ.   You said they dated for a while.

JAMIE REYNOLDS.   Right.

DET. RAMIREZ.   But they weren't still dating when Lauren went missing?

JAMIE REYNOLDS.   No.

DET. RAMIREZ.   But they still seemed friendly?

JAMIE REYNOLDS.   As far as I could tell. You're asking about them like they're my best friends or something. I really don't know them that well.

DET. STAGLIONE.   OK, Jamie. We get it.

DONALD MCARTHUR. I think we should move on.

DET. RAMIREZ. Agreed. I'm guessing Lauren being missing was a big topic of conversation when you got to school that day?

JAMIE REYNOLDS. I don't think anyone talked about anything else.

DET. STAGLIONE. Were people speculating about what had happened to her?

JAMIE REYNOLDS. That's all people were doing.

DET. RAMIREZ. Were your classmates worried about her?

JAMIE REYNOLDS. I don't know. I mean, it was weird. That she would just be gone like she was. But everyone just thought she'd come back. People didn't really start to worry for a few days.

DET. STAGLIONE. Was Matt worried?

JAMIE REYNOLDS. I guess.

DET. RAMIREZ. Did he tell you he was worried?

JAMIE REYNOLDS. He didn't actually say, "Hey, Jamie, I'm worried about Lauren." But it would be weird if he wasn't. His family and hers go way back.

DET. STAGLIONE. OK.

DET. RAMIREZ. Were you worried about her?

JAMIE REYNOLDS. I guess so. I mean, it seemed sort of out of character. But you never know what's going on with anyone.

DET. STAGLIONE.   You said people were speculating about why she had gone missing?

JAMIE REYNOLDS.   Right.

DET. STALGIONE.   What sort of things were they saying?

*   *   *   *

PAUL

I just talked to Lawrence.

KIM

How's he doing?

PAUL

OK, I think. They're trying not to worry.

KIM

I don't see that working out. They know better than anyone that this isn't like Lauren.

PAUL

They do. But they're trying to stay positive.

PAUL

I told him to let us know if there's anything we can do.

KIM

That's good. I texted Amanda but she didn't reply.

PAUL

Can't really blame her.

KIM

Nope.

KIM

I think we should talk to Matt about it.

 Message   Send

PAUL

I was going to suggest the same.

KIM

He probably knows more than we do. You know what school rumor mills are like. But I think he'll be worried. And you know he won't tell us if he is.

PAUL

I've got that thing this evening, but we can do it together when I get home?

KIM

It's fine. I'll talk to him.

PAUL

OK. Let me know how it goes. Love you.

KIM

Love you too.

📷 Message   Send

March 16th

Journal entry 5

Everyone at school spent all day **freaking the fuck out.**

Lauren not coming home last night was literally all anyone
wanted to talk about. People were whispering about it all
through every class, shouting about it all through lunch, and the
parents of the younger kids were all talking and whispering about
her outside the gates at the end of the day.

I texted her this morning, as soon as Jamie told me what was
going on. She didn't reply, but that doesn't mean anything. It
really doesn't.

It's not like nobody has ever just taken off for a night – or a
couple of days – before. There was a guy in the year above mine
who disappeared for almost a month, then turned up in the
lobby of his parents' building with a two-hundred-dollar cab bill
from Atlantic City that needed paying. He had got it into his head
that he was some kind of genius poker player and had worked
out that he could earn enough to buy a new car if he played
round the clock for a few days, staying awake on a cocktail of Red
Bull and crystal meth. It went about as well as you would expect.

I remember someone asking him why he didn't give his parents
a call and let them know he was OK, so they at least wouldn't
worry about him. His answer was something along the lines of
"This was just something I had to do for myself." I heard his dad
gave his college fund to charity as punishment.

Anyway.

I'm not going to pretend that Lauren walking out of her building
in the middle of the night and not coming back isn't out of
character. Because it definitely is. None of her friends know

anything, or if they do, they're lying really well about it. But people do unexpected things all the time, and Lauren is smart and she has money and everyone is already starting to talk themselves into thinking this is something serious, when the real truth is that you can never actually see inside another person. You never really know what anyone is thinking, or what they're going to do.

I'm checking my phone every couple of minutes because I'm waiting for her to text me back and tell me what's going on. She will do. Or she'll text her mom, or one of her friends, any minute now. I'm sure of it.

The Riley cesspit was really outdoing itself today. It's weird, because everyone likes Lauren, she's generally one of the most popular girls at school, but the speed with which people started to come up with insane theories about where she is was fucking gross to see, although not actually remotely surprising.

I don't know why I'm even giving the theories that started flying around about her the respectability of writing them down, but I'm sort of trying to get my head around this as well, and it helps to remind myself how ridiculous everyone is being.

As of the end of school today, the list of most-repeated theories about why Lauren went out and didn't come home is as follows:

<u>She had a secret boyfriend that nobody knew about and went to see him</u>

I don't really buy this one. I know she kept secrets, because our friendship was sort of one of them. But Lauren posted most of her entire life online, so I don't see how she would have kept some guy she was dating a secret. Plausibility rating: 3/10

She was depressed and ran away from home

She never seemed like she was depressed to me. But that doesn't mean anything, obviously. Plausibility rating: 6/10

She was being abused by her dad and ran away from home

I've known Lauren's father for pretty much my whole life. I don't believe he was the kind of guy who was sneaking into his daughter's room after lights-out, but I obviously can't completely rule it out. Plausibility rating: 2/10

She snuck out to buy drugs and something bad happened

Two parts to this one. I know Lauren used to do coke, because I've seen her do it with my own eyes. I don't know whether she still does it. If she does, then this theory goes right near the top of the list. Because the second part is inarguable. Bad things happen when drug dealers are involved, even the bougie Upper West Side dealers who claim their shit is never cut with brick dust or laxative and want you to follow them on Instagram. Plausibility rating: 7/10

She was abducted by aliens

I heard this three times today. Seriously. Plausibility rating: 0/10

She went for an illegal abortion and is recovering/died of blood loss

The last person Lauren dated was Steve Allison, and that's been over for a while now. So either he knocked her up just before they broke up, or they've had nostalgia sex since, or she's got someone else on the go that nobody seems to know about. In any of those cases, she never seemed stupid enough to get pregnant, but who knows? Condoms break. The problem with this theory is that I'm 100% certain that Lauren's parents would have driven her to Planned Parenthood themselves if she told them she was pregnant at seventeen. Plausibility rating: 4/10

A serial killer has her locked in a basement somewhere

Serial killers – or at least, the ones who have any interest in not getting caught – tend to target people that nobody will miss. Homeless people, runaways, drug addicts. People with chaotic lives. They don't normally pluck teenage girls off the mean streets of the Upper West Side. But there's a first time for everything, I guess. And it's more likely than aliens. Plausibility rating: 2/10

She is in holed up in a hotel suite punishing her parents for something they did that pissed her off

Plausibility rating: 9.5/10

So there you go. That's what the brightest minds at a $36,000 a year private school came up with. Doesn't it make you optimistic about the future?

She'll come back. I know she will. She'll come back and then everyone will move on to talking about something else.

She'll definitely come back.

I hope it's soon.

— — — —

March 16ᵗʰ

Journal entry 6

I can't sleep. And I sort of hate that I've decided to open this document up and write some more in it, because it feels like exactly what Dr. Casemiro would be delighted to hear, but I don't know what else to do because my parents are asleep and I already had to spend most of the evening telling them over and over again that I didn't want to talk about Lauren being missing.

They said that her parents are out of their minds with worry, which seems obvious. I'm still sure they don't have anything to worry about apart from deciding a punishment for her when she comes home, but I felt less sure lying in my bed in the dark. I don't know what it is about the human brain that it almost always goes to the worst places imaginable, that it heads straight for the worst-case scenario. I mean, I guess it might just be my brain, but I don't think so. I think it's some kind of weird survival mechanism, like it forces you to consider the worst possible outcome of any given situation so that if it actually comes true you're sort of prepared for it.

I lay in the dark with my head full of images of all the worst possible things that could have happened to Lauren until I couldn't take it anymore and put the light on and opened my laptop.

I'm not going to write about Lauren, though. Not now.

The way everyone at school behaved today kind of sickened me. There was this almost instant switch from being worried about Lauren to being entertained by speculating about what might have happened to her. It's like she was demoted from being a person, like it became about whether or not something juicy and shocking might have happened rather than about the girl – that everyone knows – it might have happened to.

Cesspit, like I said.

Here's the thing, though. *I actually like school.*

I get that that's a really vanilla thing to say, like saying that you really like water, but it's the truth. I don't hate it or love it. Most of the time, I just like it.

That's not enough for most people. It feels like every opinion has to be taken to its absolute extreme, because otherwise you're just not really committing enough, like you're failing to show enough passion or something. In terms of school, the two acceptable positions you are allowed to hold are:

I FUCKING HATE SCHOOL

You don't engage in class, you're out of the gates ten seconds after the bell rings, you mock every after-school activity, and you generally just can't wait to leave and never look back.

OR

I FUCKING LOVE SCHOOL

You throw yourself into every aspect of Riley life, you cry at the thought of leaving because nowhere is ever going to be quite so awesome again, you wear your Riley sweatshirt on the weekends, you know the school motto off by heart.

Both positions are bullshit, obviously.

Nobody really loves school that much and most people don't hate school that much. Like everything, it's about being tribal – about finding the people who feel roughly the same as you do and then taking that thing you all feel and extending it to the point where it defines you, because then you have camaraderie and you have some kind of fellowship or something. *Because then you're not on your own.*

I know full well that some of the most ra-ra Riley cheerleaders can't wait to leave and never talk to any of their so-called friends again, and I know that some of the burn-it-all-down crowd secretly obsess about their grades and are genuinely terrified of what comes next. And that's all fine, because high school is scary and bewildering and you do what you have to do to make it easier, to get through each day and get out of the bed the next morning.

I get it. Honestly, I do.

Me? I like school. But I can honestly say that I've never been happier to hear the bell than I was this afternoon.

OK.

I know I said I wasn't going to write about Lauren. But it's my diary, so tough shit.

Girls were hugging and telling each other it was going to be OK, that Lauren is going to be OK, and guys were walking around with those pained expressions that not very clever people think makes them look like they're thinking really deeply about something, like something is weighing heavily on their minds. For about the first hour this morning everyone was just acting like they were in shock, like they were just so overwhelmed, but by lunchtime most people had shifted from loudly proclaiming what an angelic presence on earth Lauren is and how profoundly they hope she's OK to concluding that she's a spoilt bitch worrying her parents for no reason in what felt like about ten minutes.

From what I've seen on social media since school let out, that's now firmly the dominant theory: that she had a fight with her parents and stormed out and is hiding out for a couple of days because she knows it will make them worry. Which, as I said in my last entry, is at least plausible.

The second most popular is that she actually ran away from home, that she just couldn't take her life anymore and has gone off to make a new one somewhere else. Which makes far less sense.

The rest of the theories – that she has gone to California to do porn, that she was a secret two-grand-a-night escort and has been taken to Moscow or Qatar against her will, that she was secretly into Satanism and went out to do some kind of ritual that went wrong – took off like wildfire around Riley. By three o'clock people were telling each other rumors they heard an hour earlier like they were Gospel truths. In last period a guy I've never spoken to before showed me a clip on his phone of a girl on her knees with about eight naked guys lined up in front of her and told me with absolute certainty that this was the chick who people were saying was missing.

I pointed out that the woman in the video had black hair and looked to be in at least her mid-thirties. He looked annoyed and asked me if I was her dad or something.

I stayed out of the whole thing as best I could. Steve Allison was making an even bigger display of himself than usual, storming around the halls with his phone in his hand and what he presumably thought was a determined look on his face, being trailed around by the freshmen and sophomore girls who think he's God's gift to high school girls, all of them clasping their hands to their chests and asking him over and over again if he was OK, if there was anything, anything at all, that they could do for him.

Lauren's actual friends clearly had no intention of being part of The Steve Show, and I was relieved about that. Elle Solomon and Rachel Kluber mostly just stuck together all day. They looked a little bit pale, and they seemed – if it's even possible – to be checking their phones a little more often than usual, but they mostly kept to themselves.

I talked to Jamie and he told me that he had heard that things were rough in the Bailey household, that Lauren's dad had been up to his usual shit and this time her mom had decided not to just ignore it and get her Xanax prescription refilled. That she had hired a lawyer and was making plans to move out. I didn't ask him how he had come by this extraordinarily personal information. Instead, I just nodded and told him that I could imagine that being rough on Lauren if it was true. He looked really pleased.

I didn't tell him about the text on my phone, the one I got from Lauren three days ago.

It came in the middle of a conversation that started off being about the History test we have next week. I'm pretty good at History, and she wanted to know what I was focusing on for the test. I reminded her that the test didn't actually mean anything, that it was just one of those check-everyone's-progress quizzes that teachers like to set every now and then, but she insisted I gave her a list of the things I thought were likely to come up and the shortest cuts for knowing enough to pass. I asked how her family was, and she didn't reply for so long that I assumed she was either letting me know it was none of my business or she'd gone to do something else.

But then she texted me back and told me that her dad had come clean to her mom about all the fucking around he's done, that he was a sex addict and an alcoholic and that he was getting help for both, that he had started therapy and he would go to residential rehab if that's what it took.

I asked her how she felt about all that, and she said she mostly thought it was her dad trying to let himself off the hook for all the shitty things he's done, but that her mom seemed pleased. That she seemed better than she had in a long while. So I said that was good, right? And she said that time would tell, but in the short term she was trying to give them both whatever support they needed.

Which brings me back to the explanations that most people have accepted as the truth. If she was so furious with her dad for the things he confessed or with her mom for accepting his reasons and not throwing him out, if she wanted to make it clear that she was angry and punish them, then why wouldn't she have done that last week when the shit actually hit the fan?

And if she was sick of her life and actively making preparations to run away and leave everything – including her parents – behind, why would she have told me that she was supporting them both and that only time would tell how things turned out?

That doesn't sound to me like the thinking of a girl with one foot out of the door. And it doesn't sound like *Lauren*. Neither of those explanations do.

She has a temper that I know is sometimes shorter than she would like it to be, but she's not the kind of person who would ever actively try to hurt anyone, who would take pleasure in watching the people she loves suffer. I'm absolutely certain that if she actually has run away, she would have left her parents a note or texted them or given them a call to let them know she was OK. The Lauren I know wouldn't want them to worry.

Which is why there's this hollow feeling in the pit of my stomach, even though it's been barely eighteen hours since the last time anyone saw her.

Because I can't help thinking that something bad has happened to her.

— — — —

Student Welfare Officer <welfare@riley.ny.edu>
To: Class of 2018 (Parents/Guardians)
Date: 18 March at 07:56
Subject: Police interviews at Riley

Dear Parents and Guardians,

As per my email yesterday, the NYPD have now officially opened a missing-persons investigation into the disappearance of Lauren Bailey, given that more than twenty-four hours have now passed since she was last seen.

The case is being led by Detective Mia Ramirez of the 20th Precinct (mramirez@nypd.org). She has asked me to reassure you all that there remains no cause for alarm, or any suggestion whatsoever of foul play. The designation of Lauren as a missing person is largely a procedural distinction, which allows Detective Ramirez and her colleagues to bring more resources to bear on the matter.

Detective Ramirez will be visiting Riley today, to conduct interviews with those members of the Class of 2018 who knew Lauren, and who may have any useful information. These interviews will be on an informal basis: however, any parents or guardians who wish their child to be exempted from this process should let me know via reply to this email. Detective Ramirez cannot rule out the possibility that certain students who were close to Lauren will be compelled to be interviewed, although I am assured that such a situation will be handled with discretion and with the full involvement of parents and guardians.

I know that this is a distressing time for all of us in the Riley family. Please do not hesitate to come to me with any questions you may have, and please do encourage your children to do the same. And I would urge all of you to keep Lauren and her family in your thoughts and prayers.

Best wishes

Jon Alderman
Student Welfare Officer
The Riley School

MARCH 18TH 2018, THE RILEY SCHOOL, 342 WEST 85TH STREET, MANHATTAN, NY

Participants:
Detective Mia Ramirez
Steven Allison

DET. RAMIREZ.   You and Lauren Bailey were close. Right?

STEVEN ALLISON.   Yeah. We dated for a while.

DET. RAMIREZ.   For how long?

STEVEN ALLISON.   About three months.

DET. RAMIREZ.   Why did it end?

STEVEN ALLISON.   She broke up with me.

DET. RAMIREZ.   Why?

STEVEN ALLISON.   She thought I was cheating on her.

DET. RAMIREZ.   Were you?

STEVEN ALLISON.   What does that have to do with her being missing?

DET. RAMIREZ.   Probably nothing. I'm just trying to get a sense of how she was in the last few weeks. If there was anything she might have been upset about.

STEVEN ALLISON.   So you can blame me for her disappearing?

DET. RAMIREZ.   Not at all.

STEVEN ALLISON. I made out with a couple of girls while we were together. But Lauren never knew about that, so it can't have had anything to do with anything.

DET. RAMIREZ. That's fine.

STEVEN ALLISON. I know it was a shitty thing to do, OK. You don't have to look at me like that.

DET. RAMIREZ. Like what?

STEVEN ALLISON. Like some asshole cheating boyfriend.

DET. RAMIREZ. You were her boyfriend?

STEVEN ALLISON. Yeah.

DET. RAMIREZ. And you cheated on her?

STEVEN ALLISON. I just told you I did.

DET. RAMIREZ. OK then. Let's move on.

*   *   *   *

MARCH 18TH 2018, THE RILEY SCHOOL, 342 WEST 85TH STREET, MANHATTAN, NY

Participants:
Detective Mia Ramirez
Eleanor Solomon

ELEANOR SOLOMON.   Lauren totally knew Steve cheated on her. Steve's an idiot if he doesn't think she knew.

DET. RAMIREZ.   How did she know?

ELEANOR SOLOMON.   One time was at a party when Lauren was right there. She saw him leave with this random girl then come back fifteen minutes later looking all flustered. And the other girl put pictures of her with Steve on Instagram and tagged him in them. She was all proud of hooking up with him, like Steve was such hot shit or something. Oh. Sorry for swearing.

DET. RAMIREZ.   It's OK.

ELEANOR SOLOMON.   Yeah. Anyway. It took about two minutes for the pictures to get shown to Lauren.

DET. RAMIREZ.   What did she do when she saw them?

ELEANOR SOLOMON.   She dumped his ass. Like, instantly. I saw her send the text.

DET. RAMIREZ.   Did Steve Allison respond?

ELEANOR SOLOMON.   Of course. He tried to say it wasn't him in the photos.

DET. RAMIREZ.   But it was?

ELEANOR SOLOMON.   Hundred percent.

DET. RAMIREZ.   Was Lauren upset?

ELEANOR SOLOMON.   She was more angry than upset. She was insulted that he thought he could treat her like that and get away with it. And she was angry at herself.

DET. RAMIREZ.   Why?

ELEANOR SOLOMON.   Because everyone knew what Steve was like. Lauren knew what he was like, before they ever even went on a date. But he gave her all the talk, about how all that sort of crap was behind him, how he was different now, how he would never disrespect her.

DET. RAMIREZ.   And she believed him?

ELEANOR SOLOMON.   Not really. But she wanted to, so she convinced herself. But I think she knew people don't ever really change. I think part of her was waiting for Steve to screw her over, so I think she was almost relieved when he did.

DET. RAMIREZ.   Did she talk to anyone about breaking up with Steve? Apart from you, I mean?

ELEANOR SOLOMON.   I think Rachel and her talked about it.

DET. RAMIREZ.   That's Rachel Kluber?

ELEANOR SOLOMON.   Right. And she probably talked to Matt.

DET. RAMIREZ.   Matt?

ELEANOR SOLOMON.   Matt Barker. They've known each

other since they were kids, and Lauren talks to him about stuff. She doesn't advertize it, but I know she does.

DET. RAMIREZ.   Why doesn't she advertize it?

ELEANOR SOLOMON.   Lauren doesn't like anyone knowing her business.

*   *   *   *

Participants:
Detective Mia Ramirez
Rachel Kluber

RACHEL KLUBER.   I don't think secretive is the right
word. She was more, I don't know. Guarded, maybe?

DET. RAMIREZ.   Why do you think that was?

RACHEL KLUBER.   There was all the crap with her dad in
the papers, about him cheating on her mom with all those
models. I think that made her pull back a little.

DET. RAMIREZ.   Did she ever talk to you about those
rumors?

RACHEL KLUBER.   Maybe once. When we were both
drunk.

DET. RAMIREZ.   What did she say?

RACHEL KLUBER.   I don't remember. I think I asked her if
they were true, but I can't remember what she said. Sorry.

DET. RAMIREZ.   It's OK. Do you know Lauren's parents?

RACHEL KLUBER.   I've met them a few times.

DET. RAMIREZ.   Did you like them?

RACHEL KLUBER.   Her dad is like insanely charming.
He's one of those guys, you know, where if he puts all his
attention on you then you just sort of can't look away. You
know?

DET. RAMIREZ. I know exactly what you mean.

RACHEL KLUBER. Right. Her mom always seemed sort of quiet, but she's done loads of stuff and she's on all these boards so I don't think she can really be like that. But I only ever met them together, so maybe it was just more that her husband overshadowed her. I don't know.

DET. RAMIREZ. Has Lauren seemed OK to you? Specifically in the last two weeks or so?

RACHEL KLUBER. Sure.

DET. RAMIREZ. Nothing seemed different about her? Nothing unusual she did, or talked about?

RACHEL KLUBER. No. She was just normal Lauren as far as I could tell.

DET. RAMIREZ. Could you ever imagine her disappearing voluntarily? Running away from home, something like that?

RACHEL KLUBER. No.

DET. RAMIREZ. You're sure?

RACHEL KLUBER. Of course not. I don't know what was going on inside her, like nobody ever does about anyone. But as far as I could tell, as far as however much of herself she let me see, no. She didn't seem remotely like the type to do something like that.

DET. RAMIREZ. OK. Do you know Matt Barker?

RACHEL KLUBER. I don't really know him. But yeah. He's in a couple of my classes.

DET. RAMIREZ. I've been told that he and Lauren were close.

RACHEL KLUBER.   She never really talked about him, but I've heard that too. I think their parents are friends.

DET. RAMIREZ.   Lauren never talked about him?

RACHEL KLUBER.   Not to me.

*   *   *   *

Participants:
Detective Mia Ramirez
Matthew Barker

DET. RAMIREZ.   How long have you known Lauren Bailey?

MATTHEW BARKER.   Since I was about four or five.

DET. RAMIREZ.   Your parents are friends?

MATTHEW BARKER.   They are. My mom was in grad school with Mrs Bailey.

DET. RAMIREZ.   Would you say you were close?

MATTHEW BARKER.   Me and Lauren?

DET. RAMIREZ.   You and Lauren.

MATTHEW BARKER.   Kind of. We were best friends when we were kids.

DET. RAMIREZ.   When was that?

MATTHEW BARKER.   Grade school. First couple of years of middle school.

DET. RAMIREZ.   You're less close now?

MATTHEW BARKER.   I guess so. We're still friends.

DET. RAMIREZ.   Is that common knowledge?

MATTHEW BARKER.   What do you mean?

90

DET. RAMIREZ.   Do other people know you're friends?

MATTHEW BARKER.   I don't know.

DET. RAMIREZ.   Are you worried about her?

MATTHEW BARKER.   Of course I am.

DET. RAMIREZ.   Why?

MATTHEW BARKER.   I'm sorry. I don't really get this.

DET. RAMIREZ.   It's a simple question.

MATTHEW BARKER.   Sure. But it's like, why wouldn't I be worried about her? Nobody's seen her and her parents are freaking out and you're here asking everyone about her. Wouldn't it be weird if I wasn't worried about her?

DET. RAMIREZ.   You tell me.

MATTHEW BARKER.   Great. Seriously?

DET. RAMIREZ.   I'm not trying to lead you anywhere, Matt. You said you were worried about her and I asked you why. I guess I don't see what the big deal is.

MATTHEW BARKER.   No. I guess you don't. I'm worried because it's not like her to disappear without telling anyone.

DET. RAMIREZ.   I've heard from a couple of people that Lauren confided in you. That she would talk to you about things she didn't talk to anyone else about.

MATTHEW BARKER.   I don't know what she talked to other people about.

DET. RAMIREZ.   But she did confide in you?

MATTHEW BARKER.   Sometimes.

DET. RAMIREZ. About what?

MATTHEW BARKER. School. When she needed help with something.

DET. RAMIREZ. Did she need a lot of help?

MATTHEW BARKER. Not really.

DET. RAMIREZ. Her GPA for this year is 3.9.

MATTHEW BARKER. Like I said.

DET. RAMIREZ. Did she talk to you about anything else? Anything more personal?

MATTHEW BARKER. Sometimes.

DET. RAMIREZ. Like what?

MATTHEW BARKER. Like if she had argued with Elle or Rachel, or had a fight with her parents. That sort of thing.

DET. RAMIREZ. Did she ever talk to you about her relationship with Steven Allison?

MATTHEW BARKER. No.

DET. RAMIREZ. Not even when they broke up?

MATTHEW BARKER. No.

DET. RAMIREZ. What about her parents?

MATTHEW BARKER. I just said she did. When they'd had a fight or whatever.

DET. RAMIREZ. Have you ever heard the rumors about her father? About his alleged infidelities?

MATTHEW BARKER.   Everyone has.

DET. RAMIREZ.   Did she ever talk to you about that?

MATTHEW BARKER.   No.

*   *   *   *

March 18th

Journal entry 7

I don't know why I lied to the detective.

It's not like I have anything to hide. I really don't.

I'll be honest, though. I don't love the thought of people seeing mine and Lauren's texts to each other. To be fair, a lot of them are really boring: schoolwork, gossip, all that fascinating stuff. But some of them are about her parents, private stuff about her dad and her mom that I don't know if she's told anybody else. And the other stuff, the weird links she sends me, the creepypasta and the gore videos and all the other stuff she finds endlessly hilarious? That's stuff I **know** nobody else knows about and it doesn't feel like I have the right to show anyone else that side of her, if she didn't. Does that make sense?

I don't know.

I haven't deleted anything, and if the investigation becomes more serious and people start having their phones seized or whatever – I don't know if that actually happens in real life – I wouldn't delete them then either. Like I said, I'm not trying to hide anything.

I think I lied to the detective because it just felt like my answer to her question is none of anyone else's business. And I don't see how they would help anyone find her, so I just really didn't see the point.

Anyway.

It was a weird experience, being interviewed.

I sort of got the feeling that Detective Ramirez didn't like me very much, although I guess I probably shouldn't read too much into that. I would think that cops are pretty good at making you think they think a certain way about you, like they don't trust you or they're your best friend, depending on what they're trying to get from you. She said my name had come up a few times, so maybe she was trying to make me think she was looking at me more closely than some of the others. If I had anything to hide, maybe it would have been unsettling or maybe it would have made me feel a bit anxious, but I don't so it didn't: it just made me wonder why she was doing it.

Because I don't believe there's any way she actually thinks I had anything to do with Lauren going missing. That would just be ridiculous.

My guess is that her morning went something like this: she talked first to the people that had been identified as Lauren's friends, maybe by her parents or by the teachers at Riley, then to the people who were in her classes and study groups, and when my name came up a couple of times – I don't know why, maybe more people knew we were close than I thought – it was a name that she hadn't expected to hear so she got suspicious. It probably goes with the territory of being a cop.

I don't blame her for being a bit of a dick to me. I guess I just wasn't expecting it.

All through the interview, I wanted to ask her where **she actually thinks** Lauren is, but I didn't want to give her a chance to ask why I was asking. So I didn't ask her, and by the time she told me we were finished I was pretty sure it would have been a waste of time if I had.

Because I don't think she has the slightest idea what's going on.

I really don't.

Sorry.

School was weird again today. It's still literally the only thing anyone is talking about, but you can already feel that a few people are starting to get bored, like they're already sick of all the theories and all the questions and now they just want an answer. Like, it was fun having this big thing happen but now they're over it and they just either want to see Lauren come back or get told she's dead so they can move on to the next thing.

Fuck.

I think that's the first time I've allowed for the possibility that Lauren might be dead.

Fuck.

I don't think she is, though. I can't. I've seen the same movies and TV shows as everyone else, I've heard the same statistics that are probably bullshit but that sound convincing when some B-list actor tells you them: that if you don't find a missing person within the first twenty-four hours the chances of ever finding them goes way down. It's been more than forty-eight hours now since Lauren disappeared.

But still. I really don't think she's dead. I know how fucking stupid this would sound to anyone who read this, but I honestly feel like I would **know** if she was gone. I'm not suggesting there's some kind of connection between us, like the way that twins are supposed to be able to feel when the other one gets hurt, or that I'm particularly in tune with the universe or some other post-hippy nonsense like that.

I just think I would know. I can't explain it any better than that.

I think we're past the point where the leading theory still stands up, though. If Lauren had a fight with her parents and stormed out to punish them, I'm pretty sure she would have been back by now, especially with every single person who has her number exploding her phone with texts and calls. There's so much noise now, so much fuss. I don't think she would leave her mom and dad dangling in the middle of it all.

I think people at school get that too. The people who honestly give a shit about her, whose attention span for drama hasn't already been used up already, talked in a far more measured way today, a lot more respectfully. I think it's starting to sink in for them, the same thing that I've been trying to pretend I haven't been thinking since yesterday.

That something bad has happened to her.

Anyway.

Jamie is on his way round. I tried to put him off, because I'm really not in the mood to hang out, but he insisted. I think he's worried about me, which is cool of him, but I also suspect that he wants to find out if there's anything I know about Lauren that he doesn't. And if that's the case, he's going to be disappointed. Because if I didn't tell Detective Ramirez everything I know, he's definitely going to be shit out of luck. But there's a new raid lair we've been meaning to team up and take a run at for a couple of weeks now and, if I'm totally honest, it will probably do me good to think about something that isn't Lauren for a few hours. I might even try and get half an hour's writing done before he gets here. I've been thinking about a new

OK, I'm going to have to leave this here. My mom just got home and says she needs to talk me.

Seriously. What now, for fuck's sake?

— — — —

March 18th

Journal entry 8

So that was an absolute boatload of fun. Jesus.

Jamie will be here in about ten minutes so I don't have long, but seriously. That was some next-level bullshit.

I went through into the kitchen and I saw the look on Mom's face and I instantly knew exactly what was about to happen: we were going to **TALK ABOUT LAUREN**.

I've seen that look on her face before, like when my fifth grade report card came in or when that nosey bitch from the fourth floor Mrs Gladding snitched on me for smoking a cigarette in the alley next to our building. It's her **"This is an official big deal"** look.

And to be honest, it went pretty much like you would expect it to go. She asked how I was doing, how I felt about Lauren being missing, about the uncertainty and the not knowing and all that. I told her I was fine – which I would still argue is pretty much the truth – and I did my best to hide how much I didn't want to be talking about it with her.

The way to handle my mom – *and I guess pretty much every mom* – is pretty straightforward: suck it up and play nice.

I mean, I could have told her to mind her own fucking business, that how I feel about Lauren has absolutely nothing to do with her, but all that would have done would have been to get me a shouting match that I could never actually win and the bonus prize of having to do the whole thing over again when my dad gets home. Instead, by answering her questions and managing to look like I was grateful to her for taking an interest, I got the whole thing wrapped up in fifteen minutes and by the end she was wearing her *"I'm a really good mom, you know"* expression.

Which is cool. Because she is, most of the time.

She's just one of those people who thinks everyone needs to talk more, that everything can be solved by openness and a frank exchange of ideas and baring your souls to each other. She never seems to allow for the fact that everyone is different, that personalities aren't interchangeable or uniform, that what works for one person is the next person's worst nightmare.

I did find out some stuff, though.

When she was finished probing me about my feelings she asked me if I had any questions, and I went for, "How are Mr and Mrs Bailey doing?"

Which I thought was pretty smart: it's a compassionate question, one that shows I care about other people and I'm worried about how this whole thing is affecting the people closest to Lauren, but it also had a shot at getting me some information that people who aren't close to the Bailey family might not know.

Mom sighed and said they were in pieces, obviously, and I guess that is what you would expect from two people whose daughter is missing. But then she told me something I didn't know. She told me the exact time that Lauren walked out of her building.

She said the Baileys have watched the CCTV about a million times, looking for any tiny little thing that might give them a clue about where she was going. Lauren was on her own, she wasn't staggering like she was drunk or high, she was dressed, and as far as the cameras out on the street were able to show, she didn't meet anyone outside their building. She was on her own.

She went missing at 3.14am on Wednesday morning.

Which probably wouldn't mean anything to anyone else, but

was pretty much exactly the moment I woke up with my heart pounding and a scream rising in my throat.

Like most of the nightmares I've had over the last few months, I'd already pretty much forgotten it. The only good thing about all this shit, amidst all the lack of sleep and the being scared of going to sleep, has been that the nightmares fade away to nothing pretty quickly, normally at least by the next morning. But that one came roaring back as soon as my mom mentioned the time. A shiver raced up my spine and I put my arms behind my back so that she wouldn't see the gooseflesh that had broken out on them.

I know it's just a coincidence. But fuck.

Mom frowned and asked me if I was OK and I told her I was fine. Then she said that Lauren's mom has basically been dosed out of her mind on Valium and Xanax and Diazepam since Lauren disappeared and her dad has stopped letting the police come to their apartment to talk to them because his wife is so out of it.

Which is fucking horrible, however you look at it.

And I think it actually hit me then. What they must be going through right now. I got pissed off with everyone at school today for seeming like they're already bored with this, for not taking it seriously anymore, but what Mom said made me realize that how I'm feeling about this is a fucking infinitesimal drop in the ocean compared to what must be going through the minds of her parents.

I tried to think of all the emotions that must be flooding through them right now. Concern that gave way to panic that gave way to outright terror as the hours ticked past and Lauren still hadn't come home. Guilt over whether they did something wrong, whether this is all somehow their fault. Hope that she'll be back soon, that diminishes with each minute that passes. Grief, that creates more guilt.

Impotence. Helplessness.

I tried to imagine all that colliding inside a person at the same time and I couldn't. Any single problem can be diminished over time, can be shrunk down until it's a manageable size. But all of that, all at once? It must feel like being under attack.

And thinking about Lauren's parents made me feel something, as strongly as I can ever remember feeling anything before. That even though everyone – the cops, the Baileys, Riley, Lauren's friends – is doing everything they can, they're not doing enough. Everyone has to do more. Because we need to find her.

I need to find her.

Before it's too late.

— — — —

Amy Linares
Did you see The Reporter? 07:52

Elle Solomon
What about The Reporter? 07:53

Amy Linares
You need to go and get a copy. 07:53

Elle Solomon
Isn't it online? 07:54

Amy Linares
I can't see it. 07:54

Rachel Kluber
I saw it. So nasty. Who the fuck writes something like that? 07:55

Elle Solomon
I'm going to the store now. 07:55

Send message

March 19 2018. NEW YORK.

DAUGHTER OF GYNECOLOGIST TO THE STARS MISSING

by Nicole Sheridan

Sources inside the NYPD have confirmed to this reporter that the teenage daughter of Dr. Lawrence Bailey, the eminent Upper West Side gynecologist who counts supermodels and A-list actresses among his clients, disappeared in the early hours of Wednesday morning.

Lauren Bailey, who will celebrate her eighteenth birthday next month, apparently left the family's apartment in the Baxter Building on Central Park West – which counts two Oscar-winning directors amongst its residents and where apartments have changed hands for as much as $35m – alone at around 3am and has not been seen or heard from since.

Our sources tell us that Lauren – a pretty, popular blonde who attends the exclusive Riley School on 85th Street – has no history of spending nights away from home, and was not in any trouble at school. The family are said to be "sick with worry" and "just want her to come home."

Parents outside the Riley School gates confirmed Lauren's disappearance. One mother of a second-grade child, who wished to remain anonymous, told us that the Baileys "always seemed like a nice family." Although she went on to mention the rumors regarding Lawrence Bailey's alleged infidelities, which have been widely covered in the press and online.

The doors of The Bailey Clinic on Madison Avenue were closed this morning, and calls to its reception went unanswered. Dr. Bailey and his wife Amanda are well-known members of the social scenes of both Manhattan and the Hamptons, and have served on the boards of a number of prominent charitable and philanthropic organisations. Amanda Bailey is currently a Trustee of the Metropolitan Opera and Dr. Bailey has spent more than a decade on the Organising Committee of MOMA.

Our NYPD sources confirmed that they have begun an investigation into Lauren's disappearance, and stated that it was too early to conclude whether anyone else is involved.

Anyone who has any information on the whereabouts of Lauren Bailey is urged to contact the 20th Precinct on 212-651-5670

Office of Administration <admin@riley.ny.edu>

To: **ALL FACULTY, Board of Trustees**

Date: 19 March at 09:59

Subject: Media enquiries (LAUREN BAILEY)

Dear colleagues,

You will all have no doubt seen the coverage of Lauren Bailey's disappearance in this morning's *Reporter*. I have been told that local news will be running the story this evening, and that several national networks are preparing coverage. As a result, I need to emphasize the following in the strongest possible terms (please forgive the aggressive formatting):

ALL REQUESTS FOR COMMENT REGARDING LAUREN BAILEY, WHETHER FROM A JOURNALIST OR ANY OTHER PARTY, MUST BE REFERRED TO THE ADMINISTRATION OFFICE, WITHOUT EXCEPTION.

It (hopefully) goes without saying that the entire institution's priority is the safe return of Lauren Bailey. However, I would not be doing my job properly if I didn't take into consideration the potential impact on Riley's reputation of a prolonged period of negative media coverage, and seek to minimize such coverage wherever possible.

We will release official statements to the press as and when we view it necessary. It is therefore vital that nothing is said in public that contradicts those statements. Mixed messages will only serve to muddy the waters, and have the potential to move this situation beyond our effective control.

I would also ask you to keep your private discussions of this matter to an absolute minimum. In this age of social media, as we are all well aware, the private can quickly become the public.

Thank you all in advance

Maria Etcheverria
Director of Administration
The Riley School

APRIL 22ND 2018, 20TH POLICE PRECINCT STATION-HOUSE, MANHATTAN, NY

Participants:
Detective John Staglione
Detective Mia Ramirez
Jamie Reynolds
Donald McArthur (Attorney-at-Law)

DET. STAGLIONE.   How did the school handle things?

JAMIE REYNOLDS.   They were trying not to make it look like they were freaking out. But they were. Everyone could see it.

DET. RAMIREZ.   Why? There was no suggestion that anyone at Riley had done anything wrong.

JAMIE REYNOLDS.   I know. That's what we were all saying at the time, like if Lauren got snatched off the school steps or someone came into the common room and took her then that would make sense. But I guess they were worried about how it looked. The school's name in the papers everyday because of something bad. You know?

DET. STAGLIONE.   Did it feel like they were more concerned about that than about Lauren?

JAMIE REYNOLDS.   I don't know. I don't think they really knew what to do. I mean, nobody did.

DET. STAGLIONE.   A missing person is a hard situation. People find the uncertainty difficult. The waiting.

JAMIE REYNOLDS.   Right. I mean, I guess. Yeah.

DET. RAMIREZ.   How were you doing at that point?

JAMIE REYNOLDS.   Me?

DET. RAMIREZ.   Yes.

JAMIE REYNOLDS.   I was OK. I mean, nobody was really OK, because there was this huge thing sort of hovering over everyone, but there wasn't anything I could do about it. I mean, I did what I could, you know? I pasted up flyers on Central Park West one afternoon and I tweeted on the hashtag and if anyone asked me to do anything I said yes. But it wasn't like I could just snap my fingers and have Lauren come home.

DET. RAMIREZ.   Did it feel like what you did made a difference?

JAMIE REYNOLDS.   You tell me.

DET. STAGLIONE.   It's impossible to say. But awareness is always useful. We had a case a few years ago where this boy got hit by a car two blocks away from his apartment, over in Queens. He had just gone out for a can of Coke so he had no wallet on him, no ID. The ambulance took him to Memorial in the Bronx. He was in an induced coma for a week. But one of the nurses saw his picture on Twitter about ten minutes after his parents reported him missing. So that was that.

JAMIE REYNOLDS.   OK. But that's not like it was with Lauren.

DET. RAMIREZ.   No.

JAMIE REYNOLDS.   Do you want to know the truth?

DET. RAMIREZ.   Sure.

JAMIE REYNOLDS.   This is really bad. Like, I wouldn't say this to anyone at school or anything, but by the end of that first week I started thinking that it would almost have been better if she had just died.

DET. RAMIREZ.   Why?

JAMIE REYNOLDS.   Because there could have been a funeral and everyone could have grieved and then they could have moved on. But everything just felt so, I don't know. Like, fragile? Or temporary, maybe. I'm not sure.

DET. STAGLIONE.   How do you mean?

JAMIE REYNOLDS.   I mean like nobody knew if there was ever going to be an end. If nobody was ever going to see Lauren again, and it was going to stay this mystery that never got solved that people were going to be bringing up for the rest of their lives, like, "Hey, do you remember that girl that went missing? I wonder what happened to her?" It felt like it might go on forever.

DET. RAMIREZ.   And you didn't like that prospect?

JAMIE REYNOLDS.   It wasn't just me. Everyone was still really worried and there were the stories in *The Reporter* and the vigil and everything else. But you could tell lots of people were getting sick of it. They hoped Lauren was OK, or most of them did, and they hoped she was going to come back safe, but it was draining. A lot of people just wanted things to go back to normal.

DET. RAMIREZ.   And when do you think they did?

JAMIE REYNOLDS.   Not for a while.

March 22 2018. NEW YORK.

SUPERMODEL'S TWEET SPARKS OUTRAGE AS CONCERN GROWS FOR MISSING TEENAGER

by Nicole Sheridan

Kayden Carter, who has modelled for Calvin Klein and Ralph Lauren and featured in last year's Victoria's Secret runway show, caused outcry on Twitter last night when she posted the following message to her more than two hundred thousand followers: **@KaydenCarter** OBGYN appointment cancelled and no replacement offered. I know having a missing daughter must suck but the rest of us have important shit to deal with too. #unprofessional

The tweet has been widely assumed to be a reference to the disappearance of Lauren Bailey, the daughter of prominent gynecologist Dr. Lawrence Bailey. Carter deleted the tweet shortly after posting it, but screengrabs have been widely circulated across social media. The model received dozens of abusive messages in response, many of which are too graphic to be reproduced here.

A spokesperson for Image Models, who represent Carter, told **The Reporter** that the tweet was "a momentary lapse of judgement" and that their client "deeply regrets her actions." Victoria's Secret told us that the line-up for this year's show was not yet set, but that there were currently no plans for Carter to be involved.

Lauren Bailey, 17, walked out of her family's apartment building in the early hours of Wednesday 17th and has not been seen or heard from since. A candlelit vigil will be held tonight at The Riley School, where Bailey is a student, at which it is believed Lawrence Bailey will speak and the NYPD will provide an update into their investigation.

Police sources told us last night that they have a number of promising lines of enquiry that they are following with all available resources. However, one detective in the 20th Precinct, who wished to remain anonymous, told this reporter that "it's not looking all that good right now."

Anyone who has any information on the whereabouts of Lauren Bailey is urged to contact the 20th Precinct on 212-651-5670

March 22nd

Journal entry 9

That was mostly bullshit, unsurprisingly.

Pretty much the entire school crammed into the Riley courtyard and held candles and lowered their heads while people talked about how Lauren is basically an angel who deigned to walk among us mere mortals and lit up our lives with the reflected glory of her perfection.

Professor Vittuzzi read from a poem and managed to lose her audience in about thirty seconds. But then Lawrence Bailey got up.

He looked like he could barely stand, but his voice was steady and while he was talking there was complete silence. Nobody was looking at their phones, nobody was whispering to each other about their dinner plans: everyone just stared at him, and listened.

He said that there was a hole in the middle of his family, and that the only thing in the world that mattered was getting Lauren home safely. He said that he knew he hadn't always been the best father, that he had spent too much time working, too much time away from his wife and his daughter. He said that he was ashamed of himself. And he asked Lauren to come home. *Begged* her to come home.

When he was done a lot of the other parents surrounded him. Most were crying and they hugged him and put their arms around him and whispered encouraging things in his ears and he nodded and thanked them but you could see that he was somewhere else. His eyes looked like they were dead.

Lauren's mom stayed near the back of the crowd. Her eyes were glazed, and a woman who I think was her sister was holding tightly onto her arm while Lawrence was talking. It looked like she was supporting her, but after what my mom said I wondered whether she was actually literally holding her up, like Lauren's mom would have just toppled to the ground if she let go of her.

Then Detective Ramirez got up and spoke. She didn't talk for very long, mostly because it didn't seem like she had anything new to say. The investigation is ongoing, it's being given every available resource, there's still no reason to think the worst, etc etc etc.

Everyone listened politely but you could tell that nobody was reassured. It's not easy to spin "we don't know anything" as good news, especially not to a crowd of parents who were probably trying to imagine what they'd do if this had happened to them instead of to the Baileys while also being silently grateful that it didn't. There were a few comments made, one or two of them loud enough for everyone to hear. Nothing all that angry. Not yet, anyway. More frustrated.

Which I can understand.

I mean, it may well be true that no news is good news. But how long can that possibly remain the case? At some point, they're either going to have found Lauren or have to admit they're never going to. And to be honest, it feels like the latter is the more likely outcome right now.

Because I don't think anyone has the slightest fucking idea where she is.

Then, right as everyone started leaving, I saw something out of the corner of my eye. I turned around and Lauren's mom was in front of me. The sister, or whoever she was, was close by, but she wasn't holding onto her anymore. Lauren's mom was sort of swaying, but she was upright, just about. She stared at me, and

I stared back at her and I didn't say anything, because I just didn't have the slightest idea what to say. And I don't know how long we stared at each other, but it was long enough that I started to be aware that loads of people were looking at us, like everyone had stopped and was watching us look at each other. And I wanted to say something, *anything*, but everything I considered sounded so fucking small inside my head, so utterly useless and inconsequential.

She stepped forward, and I had this sudden certainty that she was going to slap me. I mean, it would have been completely insane of her to do so, because I haven't done anything to her or to anyone else, but it just suddenly felt like that was what was going to happen, because in movies and on TV shows when two people are in front of each other and everything falls silent and everyone is watching them, that's the kind of thing that usually happens.

She didn't slap me. Obviously.

She stepped forward and she reached out with her arms and I was suddenly sure she was going to fall over so I stepped in to hold her up but she threw her arms around me and held onto me like she was going to die if she let go or something and her head was on my shoulder and she was crying and she was saying all this stuff that I couldn't understand, it was all slurred and the words were all running into each other so I just held her until Lauren's dad appeared next to us and gently unwrapped her arms from around me and led her away. He gave me this look as they went, that looked almost apologetic, and I didn't say anything to him either. I didn't say a word, the whole time.

And then I was just standing on my own and everyone was still looking at me and at the time I was so embarrassed I just wanted to burst into flames right there and then, but now?

114

Now I'm wondering if they were all asking themselves why Lauren's mother would hug me, out of everyone that was there.

I'm wondering if they realized there was something going on that they didn't know.

But mostly? I'm wondering what happens next.

— — — —

Steve Allison

What the fuck was that?   20:34

Elle Solomon

What?   20:34

Steve Allison

Lauren's mom throwing herself at Matt Barker. Nobody else thought that was really fucking weird?   20:35

José Sanchez

What does it have to do with you?   20:36

Steve Allison

Why don't you stay out of it?   20:36

Rachel Kluber

Why was it weird? The Baileys and the Barkers have been friends for years.   20:37

Steve Allison

OK, fine. So why didn't she hug Matt's mom then?   20:37

Elle Solomon

You know Lauren and Matt are close, right?   20:37

Steve Allison

What are you talking about?   20:38

Send message

Rachel Kluber
They've been friends for years, Steve. They text all the time. They just don't publicize it. 20:38

Steve Allison
I never heard her mention him. Not once. 20:38

José Sanchez
Is it possible you weren't listening? Just a thought. 20:39

Steve Allison
I'm not in the mood for your shit, José. Seriously. 20:39

José Sanchez
Ooh, we're being serious now? 20:40

José Sanchez
Asshole. 20:40

Elle Solomon
Lauren kept her business to herself. 20:40

Rachel Kluber
Right. I knew they were tight. But she never really talked about him. 20:41

Send message

Brady Goodman

I didn't know.   20:41

Jennifer Brody

Me neither.   20:41

Andy Lindburgh

I heard they were friends when they were kids?   20:41

Elle Solomon

They were. They still are.   20:41

Andy Lindburgh

Weird.   20:42

Elle Solomon

Why weird?   20:42

Andy Lindburgh

No judgement. I just can't see Lauren hanging out with Matt Barker. Sorry.   20:42

Rachel Kluber

I don't think Lauren would give a shit, Andy. No offense.   20:43

Andy Lindburgh

None taken. I just didn't see that coming.   20:43

Send message

Elle Solomon

Well. There you go.   20:43

Jamie Reynolds

I didn't know either.   20:44

Steve Allison

You're his best friend. He never talked about
Lauren to you?   20:44

Steve Allison

Jamie?   20:44

Send message

March 22nd
Journal entry 10

I'm going to do something really bad.

I'm sorry in advance. But hopefully nobody will ever know I did it.

Hopefully.

— — — —

Mia Ramirez < mramirez@nypd.org>

To: **NYPD Crime Laboratory (2)** <nypdcrimelab2@nypd.org>

Date: 3 April at 11:52

Subject: Entries for case number 98335/D

Physical evidence (Apple laptop computer) sent separately. Summary below.

A warrant was issued to seize electronic devices belonging to Matthew Barker in relation to the case stated above. The warrant was served to Barker's parents at their home address (see attached case report) and the following items were removed from the residence:

- One Apple laptop computer (confirmed to belong to Matthew Barker)

- Two portable USB hard drives (believed to belong to Matthew Barker)

The Deputy Commissioner has authorized an expedited analysis of these items. Please send the report to me at this email address at your earliest convenience.

Best wishes

Sergeant Mia Ramirez (20th Precinct)

APRIL 22ND 2018, 20TH POLICE PRECINCT STATION-HOUSE, MANHATTAN, NY

Participants:
Detective John Staglione
Detective Mia Ramirez
Jamie Reynolds
Donald McArthur (Attorney-at-Law)

DET. STAGLIONE. Did you know he hacked Lauren Bailey's iCloud account?

JAMIE REYNOLDS. Who did?

DET. RAMIREZ. Matt.

JAMIE REYNOLDS. How do you know?

DET. STAGLIONE. We found images on his laptop. They were copied from her account.

JAMIE REYNOLDS. Lauren posted about a hundred photos a day online.

DET. STAGLIONE. None of these images were shared publicly.

DET. RAMIREZ. We checked.

JAMIE REYNOLDS. All right. Fine. So what are you asking me?

DET. RAMIREZ. We're asking if you knew he'd done it.

JAMIE REYNOLDS. No. Of course not.

DET. STAGLIONE. Would you have stopped him?

JAMIE REYNOLDS. What?

DET. STAGLIONE. If Matt had told you he was going to hack Lauren's account, would you have stopped him?

JAMIE REYNOLDS. Why would he have told me?

DET. RAMIREZ. You were friends.

JAMIE REYNOLDS. You don't think hacking someone's iCloud would be the kind of thing that someone might keep quiet about?

DET. STAGLIONE. Maybe.

DET. RAMIREZ. Maybe not.

JAMIE REYNOLDS. This is ridiculous. I didn't know anything about any of this.

DET. RAMIREZ. Why do you think he did it?

DONALD MCARTHUR. You're asking my client to ascribe motive to somebody else's actions.

JAMIE REYNOLDS. I just can't see him hacking her. Sorry. That's not Matt.

DET. RAMIREZ. Matt made a new folder on his laptop. Of photos he stole from Lauren. I'd like to show them to you.

JAMIE REYNOLDS. Why?

DET. RAMIREZ. Maybe you can tell us why he chose them.

JAMIE REYNOLDS. Do I have to?

DONALD MCARTHUR.   No. You absolutely don't. My patience is wearing thin, detectives. I'd ask you to make whatever point you're trying to make, and I'd remind you, yet again, that my client has been nothing but cooperative.

DET. STAGLIONE.   We're just asking him to take a look.

DET. RAMIREZ.   Is that OK with you, Jamie?

DONALD MCARTHUR.   I'd advise you to refuse.

JAMIE REYNOLDS.   Just show me the fucking photos. Let's get this over with.

*   *   *   *

March 22nd
Journal entry 11

I know, all right?

I know it was a shitty thing to do.

You don't have to tell me.

Here's the thing. Everyone knows that cops are racist assholes because everyone has seen the videos and the innocent verdicts and everyone knows they can blatantly just murder people and get suspended on full pay or sometimes not even that. But if you set all that aside – *and I get that's a big thing to suggest* – then underneath there's still meant to be at least a basic competence.

Like, you get brought up being told to be respectful to cops because they're the people that you're told you go to if you're in trouble, the people that will help you when you need it. And you grow up and you realize that they're not superheroes, they're actually just people, the same as anyone else, but you try to keep believing that they're useful, that they actually really do the things they're supposed to, like solve crimes and catch criminals, because that's part of how you sleep at night. It's in the social contract.

I definitely used to believe that **(and yes, you don't need to tell me how much easier it is to believe in some kind of essential police decency when you're a straight white guy who lives on the Upper West Side)**. But now? I honestly don't think they have a fucking clue what they're doing.

I don't think they know how to find Lauren. And part of me is starting to think that maybe they don't really give a shit whether they do or not.

I mean, Detective Ramirez seems solid enough, even though she was kind of a dick to me. She definitely gives the impression that she's doing her job. But Lauren has been gone for days now and we haven't been told anything and nobody has heard about any leads or any clues and I seriously don't know how long we're all just supposed to wait for the cops to fix this.

So I did something.

OK. So. Lauren took her phone with her when she left her apartment the night she went missing. Or at least, that's what everyone is assuming, because if she didn't then it seems like nobody knows where it is it.

The police must have looked for it, and I'm sure her dad has turned her room upside down more than once. I'm sure the police have got her call records by now, even though there probably won't be any calls, because she pretty much only communicated by text and WhatsApp, the same as everyone else, but maybe they'll have found something useful.

I don't know.

Even though Lauren – and everyone else – sent hundreds of texts and messages every month and even though it often feels like nobody ever stops talking, words aren't the most important thing anymore. Images are what matter.

Photos of every place you go, every single thing you eat, every drink you buy, every person you hang out with. You can go onto the social media of almost anyone I know and piece together their entire day, almost down to the minute.

I didn't know for certain whether Lauren synced her phone to iCloud. But I thought there was a decent chance she did. Nothing would scare the shit out of her or Elle or Rachel more than the thought of losing their phone and having any photos they hadn't already posted disappear.

I don't think any of them would risk that.

I thought about it for a while. **I really did.**

I didn't just decide to do what I did, and – to be honest – I really wasn't sure it would even work. If she had two-factor authorization enabled, then there would have been nothing I could do, because I'd have needed a code that would have been texted to the phone that is missing. And that would have been fine, in all honesty. At least I would have tried to do something, and I'd be able to tell myself that.

Because somebody had to do *something*, for fuck's sake.

So.

Nobody uses their Riley email address for anything personal because it's really easy to Google what the format is and then someone only needs to work out your password and they're into whatever you don't want them into. But I've known Lauren for years, and she's used the same gmail address since she was old enough to know what email is.

And I know her password.

She texted me during spring break when she was on vacation in Italy with her family and there was no wi-fi or data signal. She was waiting to hear about her early application to Yale so she texted me her login and asked me to see if there was anything in her inbox. I don't know why she didn't ask Rachel or Elle or somebody else to do it. I guess she maybe felt more comfortable with me having her details than them, which is sort of weird. Although actually, if you'd ever met Rachel Kluber or Elle Solomon, you might find it less weird.

Anyway.

I logged in and there was nothing from Yale. So I texted her back, and that was the end of it. Until just now.

I knew there was a chance that she'd have changed her password when she eventually got online in Italy. But it was her date of birth split around the names of the two cats she had when she was little, and I'm not sure if that's the kind of password you just casually change. I mean, she might have changed some of the letters to capitals or changed the E to a 3 or the B to an 8, and that would have been enough for me to be screwed. But like I said, if that was the case then that was the case.

So yeah. I knew her email, and I knew what her password used to be.

And in the end, it actually didn't feel like anything at all.

I opened the iCloud website and I entered her details and I waited for it to tell me that the password was incorrect or that I needed to enter the two-factor code, but it didn't tell me either of those things. The site just loaded, and then I was looking at most of the contents of her phone.

There was a copy of her contacts. There were Word documents that I recognized the titles of, essays we had to write for History class and book reports for English. I suppose she might have hidden some vital secret information in one of those documents, knowing that nobody would ever look at them, but I doubted it. I scrolled past all the loose documents and the backup copies of her apps, until I reached the folder named PHOTOS.

There were thousands of them. **Literally.**

I started opening images at random. There were dozens that were almost identical to the ones before and after, where it was clear Lauren had taken multiple shots of the same thing so she could choose the best one to post. There were selfies where the angle made her look like she had a double chin or where her forehead looked shiny, pictures of cocktails where the light was reflecting off the glass, tight angles on plates of food where someone's hand had wandered into the shot, photos taken in clubs and bars that were nothing more than blurs of light.

I scrolled down until I reached a series of folders. One of them had no name, just a series of numbers. I opened it and double-clicked on the first photo.

Lauren staring into a mirror, her phone held up in front of her. She was wearing a black bra and black panties and she had a thumb hooked into the waistband of the panties, pulling one side down over her hip.

I closed the photo.

And I didn't look at the others in the folder.

I honestly didn't.

I opened a folder called FAMILY, selected all the images, and opened them. I scrolled through photos of Lauren and her dad and Lauren and her mom. Smiling, happy photos. It was weird to look at them, and not just because I knew I shouldn't be.

This is the thing that I want to make **really** clear.

I didn't enjoy snooping through her life. I wasn't looking for nudes or video of her and Steve Allison fucking or anything else that she didn't want the world to see – I didn't know what I *was* looking for, but it definitely wasn't that – but it still made me feel really weird, like I needed to take a shower. It felt wrong. **But it was necessary.** So I put how it made me feel aside, and I kept going.

There was nothing interesting in the hundreds of family photos, but when I closed Preview I saw another window open, with thirteen photos in it. I checked back into the FAMILY folder and found another folder buried at the bottom. It had opened when I clicked Select All.

This new folder was also called PHOTOS. Which made no sense, because it was already inside a folder that was inside a folder called PHOTOS. Unless it was something that she wanted to make sure nobody ever looked at. In which case, giving it a generic name that anyone looking might think was a mistake or a duplicate folder made a lot of sense.

I scrolled through the photos, and my first thought was to wonder why she had bothered to hide them.

Three of them were of Manhattan streets at night, glowing with light and busy with people. Two were taken at Riley, in the courtyard outside and in the big atrium that is designed to impress the shit out of anyone who walks through the front door. One was of Bryant Park at night, another of Battery Park in the purple light of evening. And six were taken inside Central Park, at places I recognized even though they were all taken after dark. Strawberry Fields. The softball fields near Central Park South. Outside the zoo. At the reservoir.

They were pretty boring. A couple of them were sort of pretty – the moon reflected off the reservoir in one, the strings of lights in Bryant Park were nicely centered in another – but they were mostly just the sort of photos that a tourist in New York for the weekend would take. I shifted Preview to full screen and looked at them again, trying to imagine what Lauren had been thinking as she held her phone up.

Then I saw it.

Or I think I did, anyway. I don't know.

I was looking at one of the photos of the Central Park reservoir. The path that runs around the edge, where everyone goes for their runs in the mornings, stretched up through the middle of the shot and curved away into the trees. The lights of the apartment buildings on Central Park North glowed at the right of the shot. And ...

There was something in the trees.

A thin shape, a slightly different shade of black from the trees around it. Tall, and thin, and spindly. Like a giant stick insect standing upright.

I zoomed in on the photo until it dissolved into a blur of pixels. There was no detail, just dark lines and a smudge of white. Barely more than a shadow amongst the trees.

But I knew it was why Lauren had taken the photo. I just knew.

I looked at the other photos with new eyes. And there it was, in each and every one.

A shadow, at the edge of the frame. A dark shape, thin and tall. In the deep shadows at the edge of Bryant Park, in the gloom between the towering buildings north of Battery Park. In the trees of Central Park. In the rising straight lines of the buildings of midtown.

Something barely there at all.

But where Lauren was.

In the shadows.

Waiting.

Watching.

— — — —

APRIL 22ND 2018, 20TH POLICE PRECINCT STATION-HOUSE, MANHATTAN, NY

Participants:
Detective John Staglione
Detective Mia Ramirez
Jamie Reynolds
Donald McArthur (Attorney-at-Law)

JAMIE REYNOLDS.   What am I looking at?

DET. RAMIREZ.   These are the photos Matt put in a folder on his desktop. The ones he took from Lauren.

JAMIE REYNOLDS.   I don't know what I'm supposed to be seeing here.

DET. RAMIREZ.   You're not supposed to be seeing anything. I'm just interested in whether or not you can tell me why Matt might have found these particular photos interesting.

JAMIE REYNOLDS.   I don't have the slightest idea.

*   *   *   *

March 22nd
Journal entry 12

Part of me thinks I should show the photos to the police.

I don't know if they mean anything, but Lauren clearly hid them and that means they're important, one way or the other.

More than that, they feel bad. Looking at them, I mean.

They feel _wrong_.

I don't know.

I really don't know what to do now.

Fuck.

— — — —

Found something weird. (i.redd.it) (comic_books)

submitted 1 hour ago * by breakerbreaker1989

<image.upload.photo1.jpg> <image.upload.photo2.jpg> <image.
upload.photo3.jpg>

Presented without comment. Let me know what you make of
them?
4 comments share save hide give gold report

all 9 comments

sorted by <u>oldest</u>

[-] **ririwilliams456** 3 points 54 minutes ago
Holy shit. That's a blast from the past. Haven't seen a good Slender Man shop in a long time.
perma-link embed save report give gold reply

[-] **UCDavisMAGA** 1 point 51 minutes ago
Really nice work. Post them to r/SlenderMan, they'll love them
over there.
perma-link embed save report give gold reply

> [-] **wallyworldseasonpass** 1 points 47 minutes ago
> I think it's r/Slender_Man now. They merged a while back.
> perma-link embed save report give gold reply

>> [-] **UCDavisMAGA** 0 points 45 minutes ago
>> Thanks. OP should post them on r/nosleep too.
>> perma-link embed save report give gold reply

>>> [-] **wallyworldseasonpass** 0 points 44 minutes ago
>>> Definitely.
>>> perma-link embed save report give gold reply

[-] **jamie4959packersfan** 2 points 46 minutes ago
I FUCKING LOVE SLENDER MAN. These are great. Some of the
best I've seen. Love that you've kept him deep in the shadows.
Most shops have way too much detail. Less is more, right?
perma-link embed save report give gold reply

[-] **UCDavisMAGA** 0 points 24 minutes ago

Shit, me too. I fucking devoured *Marble Hornets* back in the day.

perma-link embed save report give gold reply

[-] **wallyworldseasonpass** 1 point 41 minutes ago

Did you make these yourself? If so, grats.

perma-link embed save report give gold reply

[-] **13cenobite69** 1 point 2 hours ago

Strong work. More if you've got them …

perma-link embed save report give gold reply

[-] **waxonwaxoff** 1 point 1 hour ago

I don't see it. Sorry

perma-link embed save report give gold reply

[-] **RonBurgundystache** 0 points 24 minutes ago

Me neither. If these are meant to be SM shops, do better.

perma-link embed save report give gold reply

March 22nd

Journal entry 13

OK. I'm not remotely surprised that Lauren would have Slender Man photos in her iCloud. It's exactly the sort of thing she loves, internet horror threads that take on a life of their own and spread out beyond the person who invented them.

She makes this pretty convincing-sounding case that memes are the modern equivalent of fairy tales or myths, that get passed on and changed and told to other people until their roots are forgotten, although this is now and the internet is forever and there's no such thing as something that comes from nowhere. Everything can be traced back. It sounds good, though, even though I know for certain that when she makes the case she's just intellectualizing something she feels a tiny bit guilty for enjoying, like she has to make it into more than it is.

The truth is, she's just really into that weird horror meme corner of the internet. I don't know why she feels like she has to hide it, but it's not ultimately any of my business. And it gives us something to talk about.

I searched for Slender Man images after I saved the photos I found in Lauren's folder. There are **literally millions** of them. I made it through about thirty pages before I gave up, but I hadn't seen any of Lauren's photos by then.

Which likely means she made them herself.

We've never talked about, but I don't have the slightest issue with believing that she was secretly a Photoshop ninja. Because pretty much every teenage girl is, as depressing as that may be.

The Insta feeds of the girls in my class, including Lauren's, look like they've been retouched and polished by the *Vogue* images department. Every blemish is gone, every line smoothed out, every bulge and crease erased.

So I buy that she made the photos herself. What I don't get is why she never posted them anywhere, at least as far as I could see.

Or why she hid them.

— — — —

TRANSCRIPTS OF AUDIO RECORDED ON MATTHEW BARKER'S CELLPHONE

Recording begins: March 23, 03:31

I don't know
I don't know
I think I'm awake
But
Jesus
I don't know
I think

Recording ends: March 23, 03:32

Recording begins: March 23, 03:35

I'm awake
I am awake
Jesus
Snap out of it for fuck's sake
I'm awake

Recording ends: March 23, 03:35

Recording begins: March 23, 03:38

That was so bad

I can't stop shaking and I think I screamed but I
don't know for sure. I've never. Jesus. I don't even know.
I just.

OK

OK

Enough, now

FUCKING ENOUGH ALREADY

Recording ends: March 23, 03:39

Recording begins: March 23, 03:42

You know those nightmares where everything seems really normal? Where you're in a place that you recognize, and it isn't even weird, like everything is exactly like it is when you're awake? So you can't be totally sure you're dreaming and you can't be certain you aren't awake?

Yeah. Right.

I thought I woke up. I think that's what I thought. Because I got out of bed and everything was just like it's supposed to be. It was just the apartment, the same as it always is. It was dark. I walked through into the lounge, and the curtains were all open, which sometimes they are, because sometimes Mom can't be bothered to close them before she goes to bed, and there were lights on in all the buildings across the city and it was *fine*, it was all just fucking normal.

But it wasn't. I knew it wasn't, even though I couldn't see anything wrong, and I couldn't hear anything.

I could feel it. I just knew, you know? Like you do in dreams, the way some things are just certain, like there's no questioning them.

I knew I wasn't alone

Recording ends: March 23, 03:44

Recording begins: March 23, 03:47

I looked. I really looked. Every corner, every shadow. I think I was thinking about Lauren's photos and I guess that's what this was. I mean it has to be what this was. It makes sense. I mean, now it makes sense. Now I'm awake.

I think I'm awake

I'm sure

There wasn't anything there but that didn't matter because I could feel it. Feel something. And it was watching me. I could feel it watching me, even though I couldn't see it and I couldn't hear it. I still knew it was there.

I walked out onto the terrace and it was quiet and it was really still. There were lights everywhere, but it felt like no one was out there, like the whole city was empty. It was warm. I remember that really clearly. I looked at the park, and the lights were on there too. They stay on all night, even after nobody is allowed in. There were shadows everywhere, long and thin, bleeding into the trees. And

There was something down there. Something moving.

And I know, OK? I know what I saw in Lauren's

photos and I know what I read about and I know all that shit was on my mind when I fell asleep.

But it was there.

Tall, and thin, and black. Moving slowly. In the trees. Limbs like branches, all angles and narrow. Like it had too many arms. Or not arms. Something else. More like

No. Nope.
Not going to think about that
Not going to say his name out loud
Not now
Jesus, that's fucked
Man, I'm done
I'm done

Recording ends: March 23, 03:49

MARCH 18TH 2018, THE RILEY SCHOOL, 342 WEST 85TH STREET, MANHATTAN, NY

Participants:
Detective Mia Ramirez
Matthew Barker

MATTHEW BARKER.   Can I ask you a question?

DET. RAMIREZ.   Sure.

MATTHEW BARKER.   Are you going to find Lauren?

DET. RAMIREZ.   We're doing everything we can.

MATTHEW BARKER.   OK. I mean, I sort of assume that that's the case. And I'm sure everyone is working hard. I meant, how often does this sort of thing end well?

DET. RAMIREZ.   Most missing persons are found safely.

MATTHEW BARKER.   Most?

DET. RAMIREZ.   The majority. The overwhelming majority.

MATTHEW BARKER.   So you think Lauren will be found?

DET. RAMIREZ.   I do.

MATTHEW BARKER.   Because you have to, or because that's what you really think?

DET. RAMIREZ.   There's no reason to think otherwise.

MATTHEW BARKER.   Yet.

DET. RAMIREZ.   Right.

MATTHEW BARKER.   OK.

DET. RAMIREZ.   Do you mind if we continue?

MATTHEW BARKER.   Yeah. Fine.

DET. RAMIREZ.   Can you think of anyone who would want to hurt Lauren?

MATTHEW BARKER.   No.

DET. RAMIREZ.   Take your time. Think.

MATTHEW BARKER.   I don't need to think. People liked her. I don't know anyone who didn't.

DET. RAMIREZ.   You liked her?

MATTHEW BARKER.   I told you already. Yeah. I liked her.

DET. RAMIREZ.   Was there anyone she was afraid of? Anyone who had a problem with her?

MATTHEW BARKER.   You should ask Elle Solomon. Or Rachel Kluber.

DET. RAMIREZ.   I will. But right now I'm asking you.

MATTHEW BARKER.   She never said anything to me about anything like that.

DET. RAMIREZ.   OK.

MATTHEW BARKER.   What leads are you following?

DET. RAMIREZ.   I'm sorry?

MATTHEW BARKER. Leads. In terms of finding Lauren. What leads are you following?

DET. RAMIREZ. I can't give out any details on our investigation.

MATTHEW BARKER. Why not?

DET. RAMIREZ. Do you really need me to explain why?

MATTHEW BARKER. Maybe.

DET. RAMIREZ. You can find the NYPD Patrol Guide online. It has every regulation we follow in it.

MATTHEW BARKER. OK. Thanks.

DET. RAMIREZ. Is it weird at school right now?

MATTHEW BARKER. I don't know. I guess so.

DET. RAMIREZ. In what way?

MATTHEW BARKER. Everyone's talking about Lauren all the time and trying not to allow for the possibility that she might not come back. Everyone's really excited and really freaked out at the same time.

DET. RAMIREZ. Where do people think she is?

MATTHEW BARKER. Vegas, LA, Paris. The corner penthouse at The Plaza. Some random dude's apartment. Take your pick.

DET. RAMIREZ. Where do you think she is?

MATTHEW BARKER. Me?

DET. RAMIREZ. Yes.

MATTHEW BARKER.　I've thought about it a lot.

DET. RAMIREZ.　And?

MATTHEW BARKER.　I don't have the slightest idea. I just hope she's OK.

*　*　*　*

PAUL
Hey honey. Are you on your way home from lunch yet?

KIM
In about an hour. Why?

PAUL
John Reiser just called me. Said there was a dog going crazy on our terrace all morning.

KIM
Christ. I told her about that. I told her not to bring it with her.

PAUL
I know you did. Can you talk to her or do you want me to do it?

KIM
I'll talk to her.

PAUL
Don't fire her! I really don't want to have to find a new cleaner.

KIM
I won't. But she can't just bring her fucking dog with her. That's not OK.

PAUL
Agreed.

KIM
Did you apologize to John?

 Message | Send

PAUL

Yeah. He was fine about it, really. He was more worried about the dog. He said it was really howling.

KIM

At what?

PAUL

Nothing. The sky. Or the park. Who knows?

KIM

You'd think she'd have heard it.

PAUL

She wears those headphones.

KIM

Right.

PAUL

DON'T FIRE HER!!!!!!!!!!!

KIM

☺

PAUL

x

📷 Message Send

March 23rd
Journal entry 14

School was worse today.

The vigil seems to have sent everyone's need to publicly display how worried they are about Lauren right through the fucking roof, so loads of people were crying today and everyone kept reminding everyone else to keep Lauren and her family in their prayers, because what will **absolutely, definitely bring her back safely** is a whole bunch of people who only started giving a shit about her last week whispering to a deity who has a really, *really* long track record for letting people suffer and generally not appearing to really give much of a shit about His creation on a day-to-day basis.

The apartment was a mess when I got home.

Mom fired our cleaner today, because apparently she's been bringing her dog to work with her and it pissed all over the terrace or bit one of our neighbors or something. I've got to be honest, it was hard to summon up a whole lot of sympathy because I know full well that getting a new cleaner will take a two-minute phone call to the agency, so I couldn't really identify with the apocalyptic scenario Mom seemed to think she was describing. I asked her if she had ever heard the phrase "First World Problems" and she told me not to be such a fucking smartass. Which was sort of odd, because Mom hardly ever swears.

It pretty much confirmed that her freaking out hasn't really got anything to do with firing the cleaner. I suspect it means that she's more worried about Lauren – and her parents – than she wants me to know.

Anyway.

I'm really tired. I was going to text Jamie and see if he wanted to jump online for an hour, but I don't think I'll be able to keep my eyes open.

Screw it.

— — — —

JAMIE

I thought we were playing tonight?

MATT

Fell asleep. Sorry.

JAMIE

Are you talking to the detective again tomorrow?

MATT

Not as far as I know. Why?

JAMIE

Jen Brody said she saw a schedule in the office. Your name was on it.

MATT

Haven't heard anything. Who else was on the schedule?

JAMIE

She didn't say.

MATT

Helpful of her.

JAMIE

Don't they have to tell you if they want to talk to you?

MATT

I don't know. Maybe?

JAMIE

Seems weird.

 Message　　　　　　　　　　　　　Send

MATT

This whole thing is weird.

JAMIE

Right. You got a raid in you?

MATT

Tomorrow, maybe. Tired.

JAMIE

All right.

JAMIE

Matt?

MATT

Yeah?

JAMIE

How come you never told me that you and Lauren were still tight?

MATT

What makes you think we were?

JAMIE

Rachel and Elle were talking about it on WhatsApp. After her mom hugged you at the vigil.

MATT

What were they saying?

JAMIE

That you two were still tight. You just didn't advertize it.

📷   Message   Send

MATT
There you go.

JAMIE
I never knew.

MATT
It didn't have anything to do with you.

JAMIE
I guess not.

JAMIE
See you tomorrow.

MATT
See you.

◻ Message Send

TRANSCRIPTS OF AUDIO RECORDED ON MATTHEW BARKER'S CELLPHONE

Recording begins: March 24, 03:17

Jesus
Oh God
God
Oh fuck
Jesus
Jesus
Jesus fucking Christ
Fuck

Recording ends: March 24, 03:18

Paul Barker <pauljbarker@gmail.com>

To: Building Management <management@west85tower.com>

Date: 24 March at 08:13

Subject: Damage to terrace

Morning,

I just wanted to report some (slightly weird) damage to our terrace (apt. 12) that occurred either last night or early this morning.

I found thirteen dead birds on our terrace when I went outside this morning. I think they hit our living room window – there are smears of blood, and a few tiny chips out of the glass – and they're definitely all dead. I checked. I think they're starlings.

Please can you have someone come up and take a look? I haven't touched the birds, and I don't think the damage to the window is serious, but I'm not an expert in bird suicide, obviously!

Best,

Paul

Building Management <management@west85tower.com>

To: Paul Barker <pauljbarker@gmail.com>

Date: 24 March at 08:42

Subject: RE: Damage to terrace

Hi Paul,

I'm sure that was a pretty weird thing to find on a Thursday morning, but it's actually not the first time we've had it happen.

The Petersons in apt. 22 had the same thing happen to them last year. I did a little research then, and birds flying into windows is actually pretty common, especially in buildings like ours where the right angle can give a reflection of the park. Apparently the birds struggle to see the glass, and just fly toward what they think they're seeing. Not the smartest animals, I guess …

I'll send someone up there this morning. You're right not to touch them – birds carry all sorts of diseases – so please make sure nobody else in your family does so.

Thanks,

Steve Radson
Superintendent

Paul Barker <pauljbarker@gmail.com>
To: Building Management <management@west85tower.com>
Date: 24 March at 08:50
Subject: RE: Damage to terrace

Hi Steve,

Thanks very much – I'll make sure no one goes out there and I'll leave the terrace door unlocked. You've got the alarm code, right?

Best,
Paul

Building Management <management@west85tower.com>

To: Paul Barker <pauljbarker@gmail.com>

Date: 24 March at 09:47

Subject: RE: Damage to terrace

Hi Paul,

I've got the code.

Thanks,

Steve Radson

Superintendent

Amy Linares
Does anyone know who that
detective talked to today?   16:21

Elle Solomon
Was she back in?   16:21

Amy Linares
A few people said they saw her.   16:22

José Sanchez
I saw her.   16:22

Rachel Kluber
So did I.   16:22

Steve Allison
I talked to her.   16:23

José Sanchez
Yeah? What did she want?   16:23

Steve Allison
Nothing new. Update on the
investigation.   16:24

José Sanchez
Oh. OK.   16:24

Send message

Jennifer Brody
She talked to Matt Barker as well.   16:26

Rachel Kluber
Really?   16:26

Steve Allison
How do you know that, Jen?   16:26

Jennifer Brody
I was in the office yesterday. There was a list on the printer.   16:27

Elle Solomon
Who else was on the list?   16:27

Jennifer Brody
Just Steve and Matt.   16:27

Andy Lindburgh
Interesting.   16:28

José Sanchez
Why interesting?   16:28

Rachel Kluber
I know she already talked to Matt, because I saw him when she talked to me.   16:29

Send message

Jennifer Brody
Maybe he was getting the same
update Steve got?   16:30

Steve Allison
She shouldn't be telling Barker shit.   16:30

Brady Goodman
I'm pretty sure nobody needs
your permission to do anything.   16:31

José Sanchez
LOL   16:31

Steve Allison
Why don't you fuck off, Brady? Always
in here talking shit.   16:32

Elle Solomon
Jesus. Every time with you two.   16:32

Elle Solomon
We don't know why she talked to Matt.
So nobody start spinning bullshit about it.   16:34

Steve Allison
I'm going to ask him.   16:34

Send message

Andy Lindburgh
That should be interesting. I hope he
tells you to mind your own business.   16:35

Steve Allison
So do I. Then I get to make him tell me.   16:35

Brady Goodman
OH MY GOD YOU ARE SUCH A
FUCKING CLICHE.   16:35

Elle Solomon
You're not going to do anything, Steve.   16:35

Steve Allison
Lauren is missing. The cops are investigating.
Nobody is saying anything, and Ramirez decides
she needs to talk to Barker twice. And there was that
weird shit with him and Lauren's mom at thevigil.
But none of you think that means anything?   16:36

Rachel Kluber
She talked to you twice too.   16:36

Steve Allison
That's different.   16:36

Andy Lindburgh
Right. Sure it is.   16:37

Send message

I don't know what's happening. (i.redd.it)(Slender_Man)
submitted 4 hours ago * by breakerbreaker1989

None of you are going to believe any of this. But I don't care right now.

I've been having nightmares. Bad ones. The kind where I wake up not sure whether I've been screaming out loud or not.

For context: I go to school with a girl who is missing. I'm not going to give her name, but it's been in the papers and all over the internet, so you can find out who I'm talking about if you want to.

The cops are investigating, but they don't seem to be making any progress. Everyone is worried and everyone is trying not to freak out, but nobody seems to know anything and she's been gone for a week now. She just walked out of her apartment in the middle of the night and hasn't been seen since.

I've known her a long time. Our parents are tight. I'd call us friends.

So I did something I'm not proud of. I went into her iCloud and looked at her photos. I was hoping she might have taken some since she went missing, so at least I'd know she's still alive. But she hadn't. Nothing since the day she disappeared. But I found something else.

Inside a folder full of boring family photos, I found another folder. It didn't have a name, just a string of numbers and letters. There were thirteen photos inside it, and at first I didn't understand why she'd hidden them away. They were boring, just shots of Manhattan and Central Park. Then I saw something. A shadow, at the edges of each one. Tall and dark and angular. And I was sure I recognized it, but I couldn't place it. So I posted them onto r/comic_books because I used to hang out there a lot, and a bunch of people jumped straight on to tell me they were great Slender Man pics. And I remembered. That was what I recognized, what I'd seen before.

You can look at them at the post in my history.

The night I looked at her photos I had a nightmare. It was one of those dreams that seems real because nothing is weird, everything is just like it is in real life. I was in my apartment, and it was quiet and it was dark, but there was something in there with me. I couldn't see it, and I couldn't hear it, but I knew it was there. I knew it was watching me. Does that make any sense?

Last night I had another, although this one was different. I was still in my apartment, but the thing that was watching me was outside. We have this terrace that runs along the eastern side of our building, that looks out over Central Park. The curtains were open, and I couldn't see anything, but I knew something was out there. I walked toward the windows and I saw... something. Like a shadow, but not a shadow. Darkness that moved, that came toward me. I was standing at the window and my breath was fogging the glass and this thing was coming toward me, until the glass was all that was between us.

That was when I woke up. Or at least, I think I did. I wasn't sure for a while. I lay in my bed in the darkness and I tried not to cry because I'd never felt anything like it before. It was more than just fear, it was ... horror. In the true sense of the word. Like I had seen something that didn't belong, that existed outside of everything that moves and lives in the daylight. My skin is covered in gooseflesh while I'm typing this, just at the memory of it.

This morning my dad called me into the lounge to show me something. There were little stars of blood on the windows that open onto the terrace, and there were dead birds on the ground. Thirteen of them. I counted. Dad thought it was cool, like it was this weird thing that had happened that he could tell his friends about when he gets to work.

I went to school and I didn't mention any of this to anyone. But I had to tell someone. I had to get it out of me. I don't want to deal with this on my own anymore.

163

Because I'm scared now. I don't know if this is all my brain fucking with me because a girl I know is missing and I found a bunch of Slender Man photos or if I'm losing my fucking mind or if something genuinely fucked up is happening.

But I needed to share it. And I'm already glad I did, no matter how much shit you assholes give me for it ...

8 comments share save hide give gold report

all 35 comments

sorted by **best**

[-] **gnimel** 1 points 3 hours ago

Awesome. More please.

perma-link embed save report give gold reply

[-] **swgoh3465** 0 points 3 hours ago

The birds are a nice touch. Isn't there something about them being them the transporters of the dead or something? I think I read that in a Stephen King once.

perma-link embed save report give gold reply

> [-] **gunslinger007** 1 points 3 hour ago
>
> The Dark Half. Great book.
>
> **perma-link embed save report give gold reply**

> > [-] **swgoh3465** 0 points 2 hours ago
> >
> > That's the one! They were sparrows, I think.
> >
> > **perma-link embed save report give gold reply**

[-] **severuspotter** 0 points 3 hours ago

Nice try. Needs work.

perma-link embed save report give gold reply

> [-] **breakerbreaker1989** 3 points 3 hours ago
>
> Not trying anything. Fuck you.
>
> **perma-link embed save report give gold reply**

> > [-] **severuspotter** . 3 points 3 hours ago
> >
> > Wow. Great attitude. Fuck you right back.
> >
> > **perma-link embed save report give gold reply**

[-] **klklmng7** 2 points 3 hours ago

This is great. Gave me shivers. Post more when you've written it.

perma-link embed save report give gold reply

> [-] **breakerbreaker1989** 0 points 3 hours ago
>
> I'm telling the truth.
>
> perma-link embed save report give gold reply

> > [-] **klklmng7** 3 points 3 hours ago
> >
> > Sure. I get that. Keep us updated, then?
> >
> > perma-link embed save report give gold reply

[-] **righthererightthere** 1 points 3 hours ago

Have sent you a PM. Read it and email me. Urgently.

perma-link embed save report give gold reply

> [-] **breakerbreaker1989** 0 points 3 hours ago
>
> Will do.
>
> perma-link embed save report give gold reply

[-] **swing_low** 2 points 3 hours ago

You're screwed, OP. He knows you now. He's seen you. There's only one way this ends. Start putting your affairs in order.

perma-link embed save report give gold reply

> [-] **klklmng7** 0 points 3 hours ago
>
> Not funny.
>
> perma-link embed save report give gold reply

> > [-] **swing_low** 0 points 3 hours ago
> >
> > Not trying to be funny. You open this door, you can't just close it again. That isn't how this shit works.
> >
> > perma-link embed save report give gold reply

> > > [-] **klklmng7** 0 points 3 hours ago
> > >
> > > Seriously. Try leaving your basement sometime.
> > >
> > > perma-link embed save report give gold reply

[-] **why5not6now7** 0 points 2 hours ago

He knows you want her back. He's daring you to come and get her.

perma-link embed save report give gold reply

[-] **swing_low** 0 points 1 hour ago
Definitely. Taking people is what he does. I'd think twice about trying to get her back, though. I'd make my peace with never seeing her again.
perma-link embed save report give gold reply

[-] **JackKetchumsbasement** 0 points 2 hours ago
This is bullshit. Check OP's post history. Most of his posts are in r/ creativewriting
perma-link embed save report give gold reply

    [-] **klklmng7** 0 points 2 hours ago
    Well duh.
    perma-link embed save report give gold reply

        [-] **JackKetchumsbasement** 0 points 2 hours ago
        Duh yourself. Just pointing out the truth. This guy is some Stephen King wannabe and you're all on here sucking his dick.
        perma-link embed save report give gold reply

            [-] **klklmng7** 0 points 2 hours ago
            Grow the fuck up, dude.
            perma-link embed save report give gold reply

[-] **BlackParadeMarshal** 1 points 2 hours ago
I love this sub.
perma-link embed save report give gold reply

    [-] **swing_low** 0 points 2 hours ago
    Me too.
    perma-link embed save report give gold reply

        [-] **hgkkkm95** 0 points 2 hours ago
        Me three.
        perma-link embed save report give gold reply

            [-] **BlackParadeMarshal** 4 points 2 hours ago
            #dadjokes
            perma-link embed save report give gold reply

[-] truefan4593 2 points 2 hours ago

Next time, you should open the door.

perma-link embed save report give gold reply

> **[-] swing_low** 0 points 2 hours ago
>
> Great idea. Just hand himself over. SMH.
>
> perma-link embed save report give gold reply

> > **[-] truefan4593** 0 points 2 hours ago
> >
> > This won't stop, is what I'm saying. You can't ever
> > know what he wants, and you can't escape him. So
> > at some point you're going to have to confront him.
> > People have survived. Not many, but some. Maybe OP
> > will be one of them.
> >
> > perma-link embed save report give gold reply

[-] penthouse_sweet 2 points 2 hours ago

If you're serious OP, you have my sympathies. If you're making this
up, you have my contempt. People shouldn't mess around with
this type of thing.

perma-link embed save report give gold reply

> **[-] rogerrogerroger** 0 points 2 hours ago
>
> OK, I'm going to ruin your day now. Here I go. SLENDER
> MAN ISN'T REAL.
>
> perma-link embed save report give gold reply

> > **[-] breakerbreaker1989** 0 points 2 hours ago
> >
> > I'm not making anything up.
> >
> > perma-link embed save report give gold reply

> > > **[-] rogerrogerroger** 1 points 2 hours ago
> > >
> > > I bet you two love LARP.
> > >
> > > perma-link embed save report give gold reply

[-] XONAANOX 0 points 1 hour ago

0/10. Would not read more.

perma-link embed save report give gold reply

> **[-] breakerbreaker1989** 0 points 1 hour ago
>
> GFY.
>
> perma-link embed save report give gold reply

Breaker1989 <breakerbreaker1989 @gmail.com>

To: RightHereRightThere <righthere8rightthere9@gmail.
com>

Date: 24 March at 22:45

Subject: Hey

Am emailing you, as discussed on PMs.

Not going to tell you my name, and I don't want to know yours.
I just want to know one thing – are you fucking with me or not?

RightHereRightThere <righthere8rightthere9@gmail.com>

To: Breaker1989 <breakerbreaker1989 @gmail.com>

Date: 24 March at 22:49

Subject: RE: Hey

I'm not fucking with you. I promise.

Breaker1989 <breakerbreaker1989 @gmail.com>

To: RightHereRightThere <righthere8rightthere9@gmail.
com>

Date: 24 March at 22:49

Subject: RE: Hey

So what do you want?

RightHereRightThere <righthere8rightthere9@gmail.com>

To: Breaker1989 <breakerbreaker1989 @gmail.com>

Date: 24 March at 22:49

Subject: RE: Hey

We don't know each other, so you can take or leave this. I just
wanted to tell you to be careful.

Breaker1989 <breakerbreaker1989 @gmail.com>
To: RightHereRightThere <righthere8rightthere9@gmail.
com>
Date: 24 March at 22:50
Subject: RE: Hey

Slender Man isn't real.

RightHereRightThere <righthere8rightthere9@gmail.com>
To: Breaker1989 <breakerbreaker1989 @gmail.com>
Date: 24 March at 22:52
Subject: RE: Hey

I know that. Or at least, I know he wasn't real. I know how he
got invented, and I know how he grew into this thing that he is
now. But here's the thing, friend. Some things that are fictions
are also real. Stories can take on lives of their own. Things that
are made up can still hurt you.

Breaker1989 <breakerbreaker1989 @gmail.com>
To: RightHereRightThere <righthere8rightthere9@gmail.
com>
Date: 24 March at 22:52
Subject: RE: Hey

So what are you saying?

RightHereRightThere <righthere8rightthere9@gmail.com>

To: Breaker1989 <breakerbreaker1989 @gmail.com>

Date: 24 March at 22:59

Subject: RE: Hey

I said it already. Be careful.

JAMIE

You awake?

MATT

Just about. What's going on?

JAMIE

Our class WhatsApp was going crazy.

MATT

Yeah?

JAMIE

You really need to get back in there.
People were talking about you.

MATT

What? Why?

JAMIE

About the detective talking to you again.
People were saying it's weird.

MATT

Which people?

JAMIE

Usual suspects.

MATT

Steve Allison?

JAMIE

Yeah.

MATT

What were they saying?

📷 Message   Send

JAMIE

That it's weird that you and Steve are the only people she talked to twice.

MATT

Great.

JAMIE

Steve said he was going to ask you about it.

MATT

I'll look forward to that, then.

JAMIE

I'm just telling you.

MATT

I know. Thanks.

JAMIE

Why did she talk to you again?

MATT

Not a clue.

JAMIE

OK. See you at school.

JAMIE

Also, Lauren's family are in the paper again this morning.

MATT

Good or bad?

JAMIE

What do you think?

Message   Send

March 25 2018. NEW YORK.

MISSING GIRL'S FATHER HAS MOVED OUT, SOURCES CLAIM

by Nicole Sheridan

A source close to the family of Lauren Bailey, who has now been missing for almost a week, has claimed that the missing teenager's father, prominent gynecologist Lawrence Bailey – who counts a number of actresses and supermodels among his clients – has moved out of the family home.

"He's staying at a hotel," the source confirmed. "The stress of Lauren's disappearance has put a lot of stress on her parents. And of course, there are other factors that everyone knows about, although no one says anything."

When pressed as to whether they were referring to the long-standing rumors about Dr. Bailey's infidelity, which has been claimed to involve several high-profile women in the entertainment and fashion industries, the source told this reporter that "to call them rumors is doing them a massive disservice."

Dr. Bailey's clinic on Madison Avenue remains closed as of yesterday evening. Repeated attempts to contact Amanda Bailey, Lawrence's wife and Lauren's mother, proved unsuccessful.

Lauren Bailey, 17, has not been seen since leaving her parents' apartment on the Upper West Side in the early hours of last Friday morning. Anyone who has any information on her whereabouts is urged to contact the 20th Precinct on 212-651-5670

March 25th

Journal entry 15

Fuck Steve Allison.

Seriously. Fuck that asshole.

I mean, his assholery is so well known, by pretty much everyone who's ever met him, that I don't actually think I need to worry about whatever shit he's talking about me behind my back – I can't see anyone actually being stupid enough to believe I had something to do with Lauren going missing just because Steve says so. I mean, Riley is a pretentious bougie place where it often seems like you don't actually have to be very smart to go there, but you'd have to actually be sub-functional to take gossip like that seriously.

So I don't think I need to be worried.

I really shouldn't be.

But I am. I can't pretend otherwise.

If Steve keeps on with this shit, if he keeps telling people that he thinks the police are looking at me over Lauren's disappearance, things could get bad. The atmosphere at school, and amongst all the parents, is really fertile for the right strain of bullshit to take root. Everyone so desperately wants to know what happened, and if they can't actually have a solution to Lauren's disappearance, I'm pretty sure at least some of them will settle for a wildly unsubstantiated theory at this point.

I knew Lauren. We were friends. Some people knew that, but a lot didn't. And I'm realistic enough to know that fact will have been a surprise to some people, maybe a lot of them. So there's a connection – one that has come as a surprise to many – to build a rumor off.

Christ. I don't need this right now.

I slept like shit again last night. No dreams, thank Christ – *or at least, none that I can remember* – but it felt like I woke up about every half an hour until my alarm finally went off. I feel slow this morning, feel heavy and sluggish, like I'm getting sick even though I don't think I am.

And there's something else.

I opened my laptop when I got out of the shower and I found something on my desktop. A Word document that wasn't there when I went to bed. I know it wasn't. It's called untitled.docx and the info on the file says it was written last night. But it wasn't, because I wrote it ages ago. I never saved it in its own file. And even if I did, and I've forgotten, why would it have suddenly appeared in the middle of my desktop?

Seriously. What the fuck?

— — — —

He had no idea how much time had passed when he saw it.

Time seemed malleable inside the forest, to the point where it had ceased to have any meaning. The rain had stopped briefly, then started again more heavily than ever. In the brief moments when water wasn't falling from the sky, the air had cleared and felt fresh, before thickening again as the rain returned. It had felt like the first storm had passed, only for a second, stronger one to arrive within minutes. Which was impossible, of course. The storms that battered the valley were huge, vast sheets of dark clouds that blanketed the entire sky. They took hours to move across the sky, and it was unheard of for one to follow another directly.

But that was what had happened. Stephen was sure of it.

The trail was still there, rougher and more overgrown than ever, now boggy with mud and with streams running either side of it, but it was still there. Stephen had considered what he would do if – when – it ended, if he found himself faced with the impenetrable wall of undergrowth and tree trunks that ran along both sides of the trail, but had pushed the thought away. He would deal with that if and when it became necessary to do so, and there was no sense worrying about it until then.

Thunder rolled overhead, a ceaseless drumbeat that shook great quantities of water down from the trees and trembled the trail beneath his feet. He paused, feeling the crackle in the air in his teeth and the bones of his jaw, then flinched as lightning burst across the sky, lighting the entire forest blinding white. A smell of burning filled his nose, the electricity in the air lifted the hairs on his arms and the back of his neck. The thunder rolled again, and this time he braced himself, ready for the flash when it came.

The lightning struck with a noise like the end of the world. It sounded like it was close – too close – and the blaze of light was long and hurt his eyes. In the blue-white seconds before it faded, leaving dancing spots of red and yellow in front of his eyes, he saw the scale of the place he now found himself, saw the trees stretching away in every direction, tall and old and endless. And away to his left, where the trail made a gentle turn to the left, he saw something else.

For a millisecond, he thought it was a tree. It was tall, and spindly, composed of straight lines and edges.

Then it moved…

Breaker1989 <breakerbreaker1989 @gmail.com>
To: RightHereRightThere <righthere8rightthere9@gmail.
com>
Date: 25 March at 06:12
Subject: Something for you to read

Hey man,

I get that this is weird, and you should just feel free to delete
this email or whatever, but I wanted you to see something.

Attached is the opening to a short story I wrote. I started it a
couple of years ago, when I was bored in the summer break. I
haven't read it for a long time, or thought about it, to be honest
with you. It's a fantasy story about a local Lord who goes
searching for a girl who disappears from their village. Which
didn't strike me as weird at the time, but now – given what's
been going on at my school these last couple of weeks – is at
least a bit of a coincidence.

What's really weird is that I found a file on my desktop this
morning that I know I didn't put there. The file data says it was
created last night, and I know I wasn't copy and pasting and
saving files last night because I was asleep last night, like you
would expect.

It's an excerpt from that old story, the bit I ended up using as
the prologue. And given what I posted and what's been going
on lately, I'm not going to pretend it hasn't freaked me out a
little bit. Because it seems familiar to me, and it seems like a lot
of a coincidence.

I don't have a clue who you are but I don't know how to talk
about any of this with anyone else right now. I don't know
whether you were fucking with me when you replied to my

reddit post, but I needed to tell someone about this, either way. I guess I must have saved the file to my desktop, but I don't remember doing so. I really don't.

And I don't know what to do now.

RightHereRightThere <righthere8rightthere9@gmail.com>
To: Breaker1989 <breakerbreaker1989 @gmail.com>
Date: 25 March at 08:05
Subject: RE: Something for you to read

I can't explain this. I wish I could. All I can say is that I believe you, and tell you again to be careful. And I would suggest you think very carefully before you tell anyone else about any of this, or that we're talking to each other. I'm not sure other people would understand.

Also, my name is Ryan. So now you know me, at least a little bit.

Breaker1989 <breakerbreaker1989 @gmail.com>
To: RightHereRightThere <righthere8rightthere9@gmail.com>
Date: 25 March at 08:09
Subject: RE: Something for you to read

I'm Matt. It's good to (almost) meet you.

And thanks. I won't tell anyone else, and I'm being as careful as I know how.

STEVE

Jamie. This is Steve Allison.

JAMIE

How come you have my number?

STEVE

Jen Brody gave it to me. Problem?

JAMIE

What do you want?

STEVE

You know Matt Barker better than anyone. What's going on with him?

JAMIE

What are you talking about?

STEVE

How come the cops talked to him again. Did he tell you about that?

JAMIE

No. And it wouldn't be any of your business if he had.

STEVE

Don't you give a shit about Lauren? Don't you want her found?

JAMIE

What does that have to do with Matt?

STEVE

You tell me.

▢   Message   Send

JAMIE

You're talking crazy.

STEVE

This is serious, Jamie. Don't fuck
with me right now. OK?

JAMIE

OK. I'm blocking you now.

STEVE

Don't. I'm warning you.

JAMIE

GFY Steve.

Message   Send

Participants:
Detective John Staglione
Detective Mia Ramirez
Jamie Reynolds
Donald McArthur (Attorney-at-Law)

DET. STAGLIONE.   You knew Steve Allison had a problem with Matt. He'd said as much on your class WhatsApp group.

JAMIE REYNOLDS.   Sure. But he was just talking shit. People were winding him up. I didn't really think he believed Matt had anything to do with Lauren. I didn't think he was actually that stupid.

DET. RAMIREZ.   You didn't?

JAMIE REYNOLDS.   I said *that* stupid.

DET. STAGLIONE.   Did you tell Matt that Steve had contacted you?

JAMIE REYNOLDS.   No.

DET. RAMIREZ.   Steve was agitated on WhatsApp the previous day. And his tone in his texts to you was aggressive. Would you say so?

JAMIE REYNOLDS.   I guess.

DET. STAGLIONE.   But you didn't think that maybe your best friend ought to know that Steve Allison had taken an interest in him. That he was looking for him?

JAMIE REYNOLDS.   I told Matt what people were saying about him. I texted him straight after. But like I said, it wasn't serious.

DET. RAMIREZ.   Did Matt agree?

JAMIE REYNOLDS.   I don't know.

DET. STAGLIONE.   How come?

JAMIE REYNOLDS.   We didn't really talk all that much after that.

*   *   *   *

Breaker1989 <breakerbreaker1989 @gmail.com>
To: RightHereRightThere <righthere8rightthere9@gmail.com>
Date: 25 March at 16:36
Subject: So messed up

People are talking about me at school. The ex-boyfriend of the girl who's missing has apparently got it into his head that I had something to do with her disappearance.

RightHereRightThere r<ighthere8rightthere9@gmail.com>
To: Breaker1989 <breakerbreaker1989 @gmail.com>
Date: 25 March at 16:38
Subject: RE: So messed up

That's fucked up. But here's something you need to consider. If there's something going on here that is outside of normal – and I think we both believe there is, given what's been happening to you – then he might not be himself.

Breaker1989 <breakerbreaker1989 @gmail.com>
To: RightHereRightThere <righthere8rightthere9@gmail.com>
Date: 25 March at 16:38
Subject: RE: So messed up

What do you mean?

RightHereRightThere <righthere8rightthere9@gmail.com>
To: Breaker1989 <breakerbreaker1989 @gmail.com>
Date: 25 March at 16:42
Subject: RE: So messed up

Look, I'm going to talk in plain terms, because I don't think it does any good to ignore the obvious. So here's the thing.

I get that Slender Man isn't real, OK? I know where it came from, I know who owns the copyright. But there are things that are primal, things that are conjured up out of something real, out of something underneath the surface. People have been telling stories about the things that hide in the dark for a long as people have been able to talk, and I don't believe they all came from nowhere. I think there are things in the world that can't be explained: sometimes I think people have seen things they can't explain and they tell stories to rationalize their experiences, and sometimes I think it works the other way around. I think that human beings can will things into being, that things that start inside someone's head can come to exist in the real world.

I'm not explaining myself very well, I know. But I think that just because Slender Man was a thing that – as far as we know – started out online doesn't mean that it isn't also real. It might already have existed, or we might have brought it to life ourselves, but when I tell you that you need to be careful, I'm deadly serious. Not everything is black and white, and not everything can be explained.

My point about this ex-boyfriend is that there are influences at work that can't be readily understood. If we accept that SM is real, or something similar to it is real, just for the sake of argument, then you have to look at what people have claimed. That children disappear wherever he appears, that only certain people can see him, and – crucially – that there's an aspect of possession. That he exerts an influence that can make people do awful things, things that are against their own natures. So that's what I meant when I said that the guy you're talking about might not be himself.

Look, I get how crazy this all sounds. And I won't be offended if you don't email me again. But I believe that there are things that live in the darkness, and I believe those things have teeth. And I'm worried about you. I think you're in something that you don't fully understand, and that you can't control.

I'd remind you not to talk to anyone else about any of this. It really is for the best if it stays between us. I'm thinking about your safety when I say that. And I'll finish this with the same thing I always say. Be careful.

Please.

RightHereRightThere <righthere8rightthere9@gmail.com>
To: Breaker1989 <breakerbreaker1989 @gmail.com>
Date: 25 March at 16:58
Subject: RE: So messed up

I'm worried about you, Matt. Are you OK?

Breaker1989 <breakerbreaker1989 @gmail.com>
To: RightHereRightThere <righthere8rightthere9@gmail.com>
Date: 25 March at 17:33
Subject: RE: So messed up

I'm fine, I guess. Sort of? I

I knew people were talking about me because not that many

of them knew that me and Lauren (that's her name, I'm sick of talking around it) were friends. It wasn't a secret, like she was ashamed of knowing me or anything like that, but she was popular and that's not really my thing so I think people don't really get why we were friends. And everyone is on edge, and looking for answers that nobody has, least of all the cops, so I'm not surprised.

I guess what I'm saying is that I'm fine. Mostly.

RightHereRightThere <righthere8rightthere9@gmail.com>
To: Breaker1989 <breakerbreaker1989 @gmail.com>
Date: 25 March at 17:36
Subject: RE: So messed up

I knew you were talking about Lauren Bailey. You mentioned New York a couple of times in your reddit post, and it didn't take much Googling after that. I didn't want to say anything until you did, though.

What was she like?

Breaker1989 <breakerbreaker1989 @gmail.com>
To: RightHereRightThere <righthere8rightthere9@gmail. com>
Date: 25 March at 17:38
Subject: RE: So messed up

That's a big question. I'll answer it when I've got more time.

MARCH 25TH, THE RILEY SCHOOL, 342 WEST 85TH STREET, MANHATTAN, NY

Participants:
Detective Mia Ramirez
Matthew Barker

DET. RAMIREZ.   Thanks for coming back in, Matt.

MATTHEW BARKER.   Did I have a choice?

DET. STAGLIONE.   Of course. You could have said no.

MATTHEW BARKER.   And what would have happened then?

DET. RAMIREZ.   We would probably have asked you why you didn't want to talk to us.

MATTHEW BARKER.   And what if I had refused to answer that?

DET. STAGLIONE.   Let's just say we're glad you're here.

MATTHEW BARKER.   Who else are you talking to?

DET. RAMIREZ.   We've talked to everyone in your class.

MATTHEW BARKER.   No, I mean again. Who else are you talking to a second time?

DET. RAMIREZ.   We can't tell you that.

MATTHEW BARKER.   It will be all over the school by the end of the day. You might as well just tell me.

DET. STAGLIONE.   She just told you we can't.

MATTHEW BARKER.   Yeah. I heard her, surprisingly enough.

DET. RAMIREZ.   OK. Let's move on, shall we?

*　　*　　*　　*

Breaker1989 <breakerbreaker1989 @gmail.com>
To: RightHereRightThere <righthere8rightthere9@gmail.
com>
Date: 26 March at 16:36
Subject: Read this

Attached.

Barely an hour had passed before Stephen was convinced that something was watching him.

He hadn't seen anything unusual since entering the forest. The trees towered above him, their smooth trunks rising like the posts of some great fence, their upper branches mingling together into a great expanse of green that blocked out all but the most determined light. But despite the gloom, there was an abundance of life at the ground level. Insects skittered and scratched, birds whistled and beat their wings against the air, squirrels and foxes darted through the deepest patches of shadow. All of this was normal, and none of it was creating the certainty that had settled into Stephen's bones as he walked.

He had first noticed something as he hacked a fallen tree from the rough trail that wound a mile or two into the forest, a trampled path used by hunters to stalk their prey and villagers to collect berries and herbs. It had been nothing more than a feeling between his shoulder blades, the sensation of eyes settling onto him. He had looked round, trying not to make any noise that might scare away whatever it was, but had seen nothing on the ground and nothing in the trees above him. He had stood for several minutes, as still as a statue, giving whatever it was a chance to move, to reveal itself, but nothing had happened.

He had carried on, heading deeper into the forest as the path became less well defined and the trees became old and gnarled, listening for anything out of the ordinary, keeping his eyes peeled for movement. The feeling came again, and went again, and again he saw nothing.

Now, it was his permanent companion.

RightHereRightThere <righthere8rightthere9@gmail.com>

To: Breaker1989 <breakerbreaker1989 @gmail.com>

Date: 26 March at 16:42

Subject: RE: Read this

Did you write this?

Breaker1989 <breakerbreaker1989 @gmail.com>

To: RightHereRightThere <righthere8rightthere9@gmail. com>

Date: 26 March at 16:43

Subject: RE: Read this

I don't know.

RightHereRightThere <righthere8rightthere9@gmail.com>

To: Breaker1989 <breakerbreaker1989 @gmail.com>

Date: 26 March at 16:44

Subject: RE: Read this

OK. What do you think it means?

Breaker1989 <breakerbreaker1989 @gmail.com>

To: RightHereRightThere <righthere8rightthere9@gmail. com>

Date: 26 March at 16:44

Subject: RE: Read this

It was on my desktop when I got back from getting a drink. I was gone for two minutes. Literally.

RightHereRightThere <righthere8rightthere9@gmail.com>
To: Breaker1989 <breakerbreaker1989 @gmail.com>
Date: 26 March at 16:45
Subject: RE: Read this

Stay calm.

Breaker1989 <breakerbreaker1989 @gmail.com>
To: RightHereRightThere <righthere8rightthere9@gmail.
com>
Date: 26 March at 16:46
Subject: RE: Read this

I'm trying. I really am. But this reads like I wrote it and I didn't. Or I did and I don't remember. And I don't know which is worse.

RightHereRightThere <righthere8rightthere9@gmail.com>
To: Breaker1989 <breakerbreaker1989 @gmail.com>
Date: 26 March at 16:46
Subject: RE: Read this

Focus on the pages. Whether you wrote it or something else did, what matters is what it's telling you.

Breaker1989 <breakerbreaker1989 @gmail.com>
To: RightHereRightThere <righthere8rightthere9@gmail.
com>
Date: 26 March at 16:47
Subject: RE: Read this

OK. OK.

RightHereRightThere <righthere8rightthere9@gmail.com>
To: Breaker1989 <breakerbreaker1989 @gmail.com>
Date: 26 March at 16:47
Subject: RE: Read this

The location is almost the main character. The trees, the forest.
It's very specific. Do you really live in New York?

Breaker1989 <breakerbreaker1989 @gmail.com>
To: RightHereRightThere <righthere8rightthere9@gmail.
com>
Date: 26 March at 16:48
Subject: RE: Read this

Yes.

RightHereRightThere <righthere8rightthere9@gmail.com>
To: Breaker1989 <breakerbreaker1989 @gmail.com>
Date: 26 March at 16:48
Subject: RE: Read this

So there's nowhere near you that's like the forest in the story?

Breaker1989 <breakerbreaker1989 @gmail.com>
To: RightHereRightThere <righthere8rightthere9@gmail.
com>
Date: 26 March at 16:49
Subject: RE: Read this

I live opposite Central Park. I can see it from the terrace where
the birds died. And from my bedroom window.

RightHereRightThere <righthere8rightthere9@gmail.com>
To: Breaker1989 <breakerbreaker1989 @gmail.com>
Date: 26 March at 16:50
Subject: RE: Read this

Fuck. OK.

Look, let's take a step back. I mean, let's try to look at this
rationally, from the outside. A file appeared on your laptop. It's
related to some very specific stuff that's going on with you at
the moment, but let's set that aside for a second and think
about practicalities. Could someone have remote access to
your laptop?

Breaker1989 <breakerbreaker1989 @gmail.com>
To: RightHereRightThere <righthere8rightthere9@gmail.
com>
Date: 26 March at 16:52
Subject: RE: Read this

I don't know. I don't think so.

RightHereRightThere <righthere8rightthere9@gmail.com>
To: Breaker1989 <breakerbreaker1989 @gmail.com>
Date: 26 March at 16:54

Subject: RE: Read this
I know a lot about this sort of thing. It's actually what I do for a
living. It's OK if you don't trust me, I won't be offended, but if
you want to let me proxy into your laptop I can try and find out
where that file came from.

Breaker1989 <breakerbreaker1989 @gmail.com>
To: RightHereRightThere <righthere8rightthere9@gmail.
com>
Date: 26 March at 16:55
Subject: RE: Read this

You could do that?

RightHereRightThere <righthere8rightthere9@gmail.com>
To: Breaker1989 <breakerbreaker1989 @gmail.com>
Date: 26 March at 16:56

Subject: RE: Read this
I'm not promising anything. But maybe.

Breaker1989 <breakerbreaker1989 @gmail.com>
To: RightHereRightThere <righthere8rightthere9@gmail.
com>
Date: 26 March at 16:56
Subject: RE: Read this

I'll think about it.

RightHereRightThere <righthere8rightthere9@gmail.com>
To: Breaker1989 <breakerbreaker1989 @gmail.com>
Date: 26 March at 16:57
Subject: RE: Read this

No worries.

RightHereRightThere <righthere8rightthere9@gmail.com>

To: Breaker1989 <breakerbreaker1989 @gmail.com>

Date: 26 March at 16:58

Subject: RE: Read this

You know you can trust me, right? I don't want to sound dramatic, but I might genuinely be the only person you really can right now.

Let me know.

Breaker1989 <breakerbreaker1989 @gmail.com>

To: RightHereRightThere <righthere8rightthere9@gmail.com>

Date: 26 March at 16:59

Subject: RE: Read this

And don't tell anyone we talked. This needs to stay between us, more than ever. I don't believe anybody else can help.

March 27th
Journal entry 16

I don't think I'm going to let Ryan check my computer. I thought about it and slept on it and as much as I want to know what's going on, and as much as I want to believe there's a simple, rational explanation, I don't really know anything about him and I don't think I want him inside my laptop.

I feel like he's right about one thing, though. I don't feel like I can talk about any of this with anyone else. I don't know how I feel about that, to be honest. It's like

Shit.

My mom's calling me. Something about the paper.

What are the odds that this is good news?

Long?

Zero?

— — — —

SOURCES CLAIM POLICE ARE "TAKING A CLOSE LOOK" AT MISSING GIRL'S CLASSMATE

by Nicole Sheridan

A classmate of Lauren Bailey has claimed that detectives investigating the disappearance of the teenager are "taking a close look" at a Riley School students.

Speaking on the condition of anonymity, the student gave this reporter the name of a male student in the Senior class who is known to have connections to Lauren Bailey.

"Nobody wants to believe that he actually had anything to do with Lauren's disappearance," said the student. "But everyone knows that the cops have interviewed him more than anyone else, and everyone knows he was obsessed with Lauren."

"They never really hung out together," confirmed the source. "Lauren was one of the most popular girls at school, and the guy I'm talking about just wasn't. Like, at all. People say they were friends, but that doesn't make any sense to me. I don't see why she would have wasted her time with him."

On the advice of our legal department, I am not publishing the student's name.

Sources in the 20th Precinct refused to comment on the claims, although they did acknowledge that the student in question had been interviewed "as a matter of routine" by detectives investigating Lauren Bailey's disappearance.

The seventeen-year-old, whose father is the renowned gynecologist Dr. Lawrence Bailey, has not been seen since leaving her parents' apartment on the Upper West Side in the early hours of last Friday morning. Anyone who has any information on her whereabouts is urged to contact the 20th Precinct on 212-651-5670

JAMIE
Have you seen it?

MATT
Yeah. I've seen it.

MATT
Does everyone know
it's me they're talking about?

JAMIE
I think so. Sorry.

JAMIE
Matt?

📷   Message   Send

Office of Administration <admin@riley.ny.edu>

To: ALL PARENTS, ALL FACULTY, Board of Trustees

Date: 27 March at 08:12

Subject: Story in today's Reporter

Dear Parents and Colleagues,

I want to assure everyone that an immediate investigation has been opened into the despicable and inflammatory story that ran in this morning's Page Six column, and that we have already sought legal advice on any and all possible avenues that may exist against the publishers of the "newspaper" in question.

It is not yet clear whether Riley students actually spoke to the author of the piece. If that turns out to be the case, please be assured that appropriate disciplinary procedures will be brought immediately: anyone found to have cooperated in this sorry excuse for journalism will be in breach of the Honor Code that each and every Riley students signs up to on their first day.

We will not allow the good name of any student to be sullied by innuendo and unproven gossip, and we will defend the reputation of this institution with great vigor.

I find it remarkable that previous advice regarding the media and the disappearance of Lauren Bailey could possibly need repeating, but so be it:

ALL REQUESTS FOR COMMENT REGARDING LAUREN BAILEY, WHETHER FROM A JOURNALIST OR ANY OTHER PARTY, MUST BE REFERRED TO THE ADMINISTRATION OFFICE, WITHOUT EXCEPTION.

The administration will continue to provide updates on the police response to Lauren's disappearance when appropriate, and will also update all parents on the results of our investigation into this morning's disappointing incident.

As always, if you have any questions or seek further assurance, please contact the admin office.

Thank you all

Dr. Jacob Heighway
Principal
The Riley School

Elle Solomon

What the fuck, Steve?   08:31

José Sanchez

Seriously. What were you thinking?   08:31

Steve Allison

What's the problem?   08:31

Andy Lindburgh

If you don't know you're even dumber
than I thought.   08:32

Steve Allison

Yawn.   08:32

Elle Solomon

Are you denying you told that
bullshit story to the reporter?   08:33

Steve Allison

Are you a cop?   08:33

Elle Solomon

Obviously not.   08:33

Steve Allison

Then I don't have to answer your
questions.   08:34

Send message

Steve Allison

And you can believe what you want. The article is the truth.   08:35

Andy Lindburgh

You don't have any idea why the cops talked to Matt a second time. LIKE THEY DID WITH YOU, YOU DICKHEAD.   08:35

Steve Allison

Last warning Andy.   08:36

Elle Solomon

You fucking child. What is this really about, Steve? And don't say Lauren.   08:38

Steve Allison

I'll talk to whoever I want, whenever I want. Tough shit if you don't like it.   08:40

José Sanchez

They'll suspend you if they find out.   08:41

Elle Solomon

Which they will. I guarantee that.   08:42

Steve Allison

I don't give a fuck if they do.   08:43

Send message

Participants:
Detective John Staglione
Detective Mia Ramirez
Jamie Reynolds
Donald McArthur (Attorney-at-Law)

DET. STAGLIONE. You texted Matt the morning that the
story ran in *The Reporter*?

JAMIE REYNOLDS. Yeah. I asked if he'd seen it.

DET. RAMIREZ. Had he?

JAMIE REYNOLDS. He said so.

DET. RAMIREZ. Did he say anything about it?

JAMIE REYNOLDS. Just that he'd seen it.

DET. STAGLIONE. What did you think when you read it?

JAMIE REYNOLDS. I thought it was bullshit. And I
thought it was fucking cowardly.

DET. RAMIREZ. Cowardly?

JAMIE REYNOLDS. Everyone knew who'd talked to the
reporter. But Steve didn't even have the balls to let the
reporter use his name, because he knew what he was saying
was shit.

DET. STAGLIONE. It was shit?

JAMIE REYNOLDS. Of course.

DET. RAMIREZ.   Was that what people were saying when you got to school that day?

JAMIE REYNOLDS.   Most of them.

DET. STAGLIONE.   Not everyone?

JAMIE REYNOLDS.   No.

DET. RAMIREZ.   So some people believed the assertion in the paper? That Matt might have had something to do with Lauren's disappearance?

JAMIE REYNOLDS.   Yeah. But some people are morons. And they looked pretty stupid later, didn't they?

DET. STAGLIONE.   We'll get to that. How was Matt?

JAMIE REYNOLDS.   What do you mean?

DET. RAMIREZ.   He went to school the day the story ran. Did that surprise you?

JAMIE REYNOLDS.   Why wouldn't he have gone?

DET. RAMIREZ.   It must have been hard for him. He must have known that it was all anyone was going to be talking about.

JAMIE REYNOLDS.   He didn't do anything wrong. Why should he have hidden?

DET. RAMIREZ.   Nobody's saying he should have.

DET. STAGLIONE.   So how was he? At school that day?

JAMIE REYNOLDS.   I didn't talk to him.

DET. STAGLIONE.   You were his best friend.

JAMIE REYNOLDS.   I didn't not talk to him on purpose. I wanted to. The opportunity just didn't come up.

DET. RAMIREZ.   But you saw him?

JAMIE REYNOLDS.   Yes.

DET. STAGLIONE.   And he seemed OK? Like his normal self?

JAMIE REYNOLDS.   He seemed fine to me.

*　　*　　*　　*

March 27th
Journal entry 17

What a fucking day. Jesus.

I nearly walked out after first period. I saw at least half a dozen showing other people copies of the article in _The Reporter_, and everywhere I went I had that thing where you can tell people were talking about you until really recently, like there's not enough conversation happening for it to feel normal, so you know that everyone has just stopped talking about whatever they were talking about and the only thing that's different is that you've just walked into earshot.

I wanted to walk out, but I didn't. Because I know how that would have looked. It would have looked like

— — — —

March 27th
Journal entry 18

Great moment for my laptop to crash. I love my Pro, but honestly, it sometimes feel like playing roulette, like any second the fans are going to suddenly start whirring and the cursor's going to freeze and then you have that agonizing wait to see whether it's going to start moving again or whether you're going to be pressing the power button and trying to remember the last time you saved whatever you're working on.

Anyway. Second period was

— — — —

March 27ᵗʰ

Journal entry 19

Seriously, what the fuck?

Everything froze again, so I held down power until I heard the fans shut off and then booted it back up. Everything seemed fine after I logged in, but then the cursor started stuttering when I moved the trackpad, like it was lagging, and I don't know why but I noticed that Dropbox looked different, like it was a slightly different icon design, so I right-clicked it and Dropbox wasn't there. Instead there was just this little almost-Dropbox icon and a string of letters and numbers. So I checked the activity log and this thing, whatever it is, is running in the background at all times, and is set to open on start-up. I dug through preferences until I found it, and the option to turn it off is greyed out.

I googled the random string of characters, and the first result that came up was a forum post from some goofy spy website, the kind of place where you can buy night-vision goggles and cameras the size of buttons and apps you can download onto your wife's phone so you can track everything she does when you're at work.

The post was offering a free download of something called a Keystrokes Recorder. Apparently you load it onto a computer and it records every key that gets pressed and emails a transcript to whichever address you enter.

I don't know how long it's been there. I don't know if it just appeared, or if I just didn't notice until just now.

I don't know where the fuck it came from. And I want to tell myself I don't know who put it there, but I think I do.

Fuck.

— — — —

Breaker1989 <breakerbreaker1989 @gmail.com>
To: RightHereRightThere <righthere8rightthere9@gmail.com>
Date: 27 March at 18:09
Subject: Did you put something on my laptop?

Tell me the truth.

RightHereRightThere <righthere8rightthere9@gmail.com>
To: Breaker1989 <breakerbreaker1989 @gmail.com>
Date: 27 March at 18:11
Subject: RE: Did you put something on my laptop?

What are you talking about?

Breaker1989 <breakerbreaker1989 @gmail.com>
To: RightHereRightThere <righthere8rightthere9@gmail.com>
Date: 27 March at 18:12
Subject: RE: Did you put something on my laptop?

If you did it, then you know.

RightHereRightThere <righthere8rightthere9@gmail.com>
To: Breaker1989 <breakerbreaker1989 @gmail.com>
Date: 27 March at 18:13
Subject: RE: Did you put something on my laptop?

Are we doing riddles now? Because I don't know what you're talking about. Are you OK, Matt? I'm getting worried.

Breaker1989 <breakerbreaker1989 @gmail.com>
To: RightHereRightThere <righthere8rightthere9@gmail.com>
Date: 27 March at 18:15
Subject: RE: Did you put something on my laptop?

___

I found something on my laptop. It's been recording what I do. Which is quite a coincidence after you asked me to give you access and you told me you know a lot about this sort of thing.

RightHereRightThere <righthere8rightthere9@gmail.com>
To: Breaker1989 <breakerbreaker1989 @gmail.com>
Date: 27 March at 18:18
Subject: RE: Did you put something on my laptop?

___

Are you listening to yourself? How could I have installed something onto your laptop? I'd need your IP address, I'd need to know your system password.

This isn't like you, Matt. You're not thinking straight and with everything that's going on I totally get why, but I'm still worried. Tell me what you found.

Breaker1989 <breakerbreaker1989 @gmail.com>
To: RightHereRightThere <righthere8rightthere9@gmail.com>
Date: 27 March at 18:20
Subject: RE: Did you put something on my laptop?

___

You don't know what's "like me" and what "isn't". You don't know me at all.

RightHereRightThere <righthere8rightthere9@gmail.com>
To: Breaker1989 <breakerbreaker1989 @gmail.com>
Date: 27 March at 18:21
Subject: RE: Did you put something on my laptop?

Matt, come on. We're friends. We're in this together.

RightHereRightThere <righthere8rightthere9@gmail.com>
To: Breaker1989 <breakerbreaker1989 @gmail.com>
Date: 27 March at 18:23
Subject: RE: Did you put something on my laptop?

Don't shut me out, Matt. You can't do this on your own. You
need me.

RightHereRightThere <righthere8rightthere9@gmail.com>
To: Breaker1989 <breakerbreaker1989 @gmail.com>
Date: 27 March at 18:26
Subject: RE: Did you put something on my laptop?

Fine. FUCK YOU. I hope he fucking takes you like he took that
bitch friend of yours.

March 27th
Journal entry 20

Fuck that guy.

I tried to get rid of the thing that was pretending to be Dropbox but I couldn't drag it to the trash and I couldn't delete it out of applications so I ended up buying an uninstaller out of the app store and that got rid of it. At least, it looks like it did. I guess I don't know, because there's nothing running in the background anymore but for all I know it might just hide itself better if you manage to delete it once.

It might still be there. It might be recording me pressing the keys to type this sentence.

Actually, at this point, fuck everything. I'm going to bed.

— — — —

March 28th
Journal entry 21

I'm so cold.

My arms are shaking and my fingers are blue and I'm supposed to go to school in an hour but I stood in the shower for almost twenty minutes and I just can't get warm. I keep having to hit delete because my fingers are shaking too much to hit the right keys.

I can't stop crying, either.

I cried in the shower, where I hoped nobody could hear me. I cried because I'm scared and it feels like my mind is coming unglued, like something has taken hold of it and twisted it and tilted it and put it back inside my head and now it doesn't work properly anymore and

OK. OK.

It's OK. It's daylight and I'm back inside and I'm OK. I think I'm OK.

Last night

Jesus. I don't even know how to

I think I was asleep. But I don't even know if that matters anymore.

— — — —

It's getting worse. (i.redd.it)(Slender_Man)

submitted 1 hour ago * by breakerbreaker1989

There was an article in a newspaper about me yesterday. Some people I go to school with told a reporter that the cops think I have something to do with the girl who went missing (see my previous posts for context).

I would never, ever have hurt her. Not knowingly, at least. But there are gaps. Black holes in my head when I can't remember anything, and one of them is the night she went missing. So I don't know.

I don't know anything anymore.

Last night I was standing on our terrace that looks out over Central Park. I think I knew I was asleep, because the city didn't look right. The park was black. There are lights that stay on all night, because police go in and out all the time to stop people sleeping there, but they were all off. It was this dark rectangle, like something was casting some huge shadow over it.

I remember looking at the buildings that overlook the park, and they were dark too. I could see lights in the distance, but everything was black around the park, like something had turned the city off for about three blocks in every direction.

Then I saw a light. At the north end of the park, near where the reservoir is, there was this tiny pinprick of blue light. I stared at it, and I wanted to go to it, but I couldn't move. Everything was silent and everything was still and I couldn't move and the light just stayed where it was, tiny and bright in the middle of a sea of darkness.

I woke up on the terrace. I was freezing cold, shivering. But the city looked normal again. There were people running in the park and cars on the streets and it was noisy and it was just a normal morning.

The blue light was gone. Or maybe I just couldn't see it in daylight.

I turned around to go inside and get ready for school, and I saw it.

218

On the wall, on the pale stone. A figure.

It was tall and thin, with long limbs. It towered over me, and even though I saw that it wasn't alive, that it was just an outline, I knew that it was looking at me. I just knew.

I walked over and touched it. It smeared under my fingers, then started to blow away. Black dust, like ash. Like something had been stood over me while I slept, then left an imprint of itself behind when the sun came up.

My skin was crawling. My arms were covered in gooseflesh, and I knew it was because I was cold.

I took the hosepipe and I washed it away. But I can still see it. When I close my eyes, I can see it so clearly.

8 comments share save hide give gold report

all 5 comments

sorted by **best**

[-] **jkkhh** 0 points 1 hour ago
Chills. Bravo.
perma-link embed save report give gold reply

[-] **righthererightthere** 0 points 1 hour ago
Check your email.
perma-link embed save report give gold reply

[-] **crouch_end55** 0 points 1 hour ago
The blue light is the missing girl, right?
perma-link embed save report give gold reply

> [-] **jkkkhh** 0 points 1 hour ago
> Obvs.
> **perma-link embed save report give gold reply**

[-] **vic32shaker** 1 points 1 hour ago
More. ASAP. I love this.
perma-link embed save report give gold reply

RightHereRightThere <righthere8rightthere9@gmail.com>
To: Breaker1989 <breakerbreaker1989 @gmail.com>
Date: 28 March at 10:02
Subject: Your new post

Are you OK?

RightHereRightThere <righthere8rightthere9@gmail.com>
To: Breaker1989 <breakerbreaker1989 @gmail.com>
Date: 28 March at 10:10
Subject: RE: Your new post

I don't know what was going on with you yesterday. And I'm
sorry for what I said. I was angry, because I've only ever tried to
help you and support you. So what you accused me of hurt. I
shouldn't have lashed out, though. I take it back.

RightHereRightThere <righthere8rightthere9@gmail.com>
To: Breaker1989 <breakerbreaker1989 @gmail.com>
Date: 28 March at 10:12
Subject: RE: Your new post

You don't have to get into this. Just let me know you're OK.

Please.

Breaker1989 <breakerbreaker1989 @gmail.com>
To: RightHereRightThere <righthere8rightthere9@gmail.
com>
Date: 28 March at 12:31
Subject: RE: Your new post

I've been better.

220

RightHereRightThere <righthere8rightthere9@gmail.com>
To: Breaker1989 <breakerbreaker1989 @gmail.com>
Date: 28 March at 12:33
Subject: RE: Your new post

I bet. Good to hear from you, man. I thought you'd dropped me.

Breaker1989 <breakerbreaker1989 @gmail.com>
To: RightHereRightThere <righthere8rightthere9@gmail. com>
Date: 28 March at 12:33
Subject: RE: Your new post

I appreciate you taking back what you wrote. And I guess I have to trust you. I don't have anyone else right now.

RightHereRightThere <righthere8rightthere9@gmail.com>
To: Breaker1989 <breakerbreaker1989 @gmail.com>
Date: 28 March at 12:34
Subject: RE: Your new post

Hang in there. You'll be OK.

What are you going to do?

Breaker1989 <breakerbreaker1989 @gmail.com>
To: RightHereRightThere <righthere8rightthere9@gmail. com>
Date: 28 March at 12:36
Subject: RE: Your new post

I have to get Lauren back. I understand that now. I have to do it for myself, because people are talking about me now and it's only going to get worse. But more than that, I have to get her back because I'm starting to think that I'm the only one who can.

RightHereRightThere <righthere8rightthere9@gmail.com>
To: Breaker1989 <breakerbreaker1989 @gmail.com>
Date: 28 March at 12:37
Subject: Your new post

The blue light.

Breaker1989 <breakerbreaker1989 @gmail.com>
To: RightHereRightThere <righthere8rightthere9@gmail.com>
Date: 28 March at 12:39
Subject: RE: Your new post

Yeah. That's where she is. I wasn't sure, even after what I saw last night, but then this was on my desktop this morning. Read it.

Stephen frowned.

For the last minute or so, he had been hearing a sound. The forest was soaked with rain, and the dripping from branches and leaves was a constant cacophony. The sound he had been hearing was underneath all that, and was also water, but had made no sense. It had been the soft lapping of waves, as though he was within earshot of the sea.

Which was ridiculous, of course. The nearest coastline was six weeks' solid hiking east along the winding path of the river that ran through the village.

He walked up through the undergrowth, and stopped. For the longest moment, he simply could not believe what his eyes were seeing.

Stretching out before him was a lake. It was not huge – he could see the banks all the way around – but it was far bigger than anything he had ever heard of existing inside the forest. He had heard no stories of a lake from the hunters or trappers who spent more time inside the forest than anyone, and it would never have occurred to him to wonder. There were no rivers that passed through the forest, so a lake should have been an impossibility. A rain-water pond, perhaps, but what he was looking at was not that. There was simply too much water, and it was bright and clear in the starlight, not the brackish murk of a stagnant pool.

Stephen looked around. The trail – such as it had been at the end – ended here, but there was a trampled path running along the water's edge. It appeared to go all the way around the lake. For all he knew, the trail reappeared on the far side, heading ever deeper into the forest, but he didn't think so.

He suspected this was the end of the road.

RightHereRightThere <righthere8rightthere9@gmail.com>
To: Breaker1989 <breakerbreaker1989 @gmail.com>
Date: 28 March at 12:30
Subject: Your new post

Holy shit. The lake is the Central Park reservoir, right?

Breaker1989 <breakerbreaker1989 @gmail.com>
To: RightHereRightThere <righthere8rightthere9@gmail.com>
Date: 28 March at 12:31
Subject: RE: Your new post

I think so. It has to be.

RightHereRightThere <righthere8rightthere9@gmail.com>
To: Breaker1989 <breakerbreaker1989 @gmail.com>
Date: 28 March at 12:32
Subject: RE: Your new post

I'm begging you to be careful, my friend. I get that you have to
do this, and I think you're right, for whatever that's worth, but this
is really, really serious. If SM has her, and if he's challenging you
to get her back, there'll be a cost. He won't let her go easily.

Breaker1989 <breakerbreaker1989 @gmail.com>
To: RightHereRightThere <righthere8rightthere9@gmail.com>
Date: 28 March at 12:32
Subject: RE: Your new post

I'll be careful.

RightHereRightThere <righthere8rightthere9@gmail.com>

To: Breaker1989 <breakerbreaker1989 @gmail.com>

Date: 28 March at 12:34

Subject: RE: Your new post

You're doing the right thing. You're a fucking hero.

Breaker1989 <breakerbreaker1989 @gmail.com>

To: RightHereRightThere <righthere8rightthere9@gmail.
com>

Date: 28 March at 12:34

Subject: RE: Your new post

I have to go.

TRANSCRIPTS OF AUDIO RECORDED ON PAUL BARKER'S CELLPHONE

Recording begins: March 28, 19:17

KIMBERLEY BARKER: We should do this more often. Don't you think?

MATTHEW BARKER: Do what, Mom?

KIMBERLEY BARKER: Have dinner together. At a table, like a regular family.

PAUL BARKER: We should.

MATTHEW BARKER: Why?

KIMBERLEY BARKER: What do you mean, why?

MATTHEW BARKER: Why does it matter if we sit at the table or not? If you want us to hang out and talk, we can do that in the lounge.

KIMBERLEY BARKER: Because there's something nice about sitting together without the TV on.

MATTHEW BARKER: I guess so.

PAUL BARKER: I think your mother's right. We should try to make more of an effort. I know we're all busy, but you have to try and make time.

MATTHEW BARKER: Maybe you and I can put tuxedos on and Mom can wear a cocktail dress?

PAUL BARKER: Don't be a smartass, Matthew.

MATTHEW BARKER: Funny.

PAUL BARKER: What is?

MATTHEW BARKER: That you call me Matthew when you're annoyed with me. It's such a cliché.

PAUL BARKER: Don't be annoying and I won't have to call you Matthew.

MATTHEW BARKER: Fair enough.

KIMBERLEY BARKER: Anyway. How was your day, Matt?

MATTHEW BARKER: Fine, I guess. Everyone is still going crazy about that thing in *The Reporter*.

PAUL BARKER: I bet. We got an email from Dr. Heighway this morning. I think it's fair to say he isn't happy.

MATTHEW BARKER: He's just worried about anything that might make Riley look bad. He doesn't really care about Lauren being missing.

KIMBERLEY BARKER: You don't know that. That's an awful thing to say.

MATTHEW BARKER: It's the truth.

PAUL BARKER: Based on what?

MATTHEW BARKER: Forget it. Sorry I said anything.

KIMBERLEY BARKER: No, tell us. You don't think the school cares about finding Lauren?

MATTHEW BARKER: I'm sure they do, but only because that will make the story go away. Right now they're the expensive private school who has that student who went missing. It's not a great look.

KIMBERLEY BARKER: She didn't go missing from school.

MATTHEW BARKER: I know that.

KIMBERLEY BARKER: So, I guess I don't see how this makes Riley look bad.

MATTHEW BARKER: I don't think it does either. But they clearly do.

PAUL BARKER: Do they know who talked to that reporter yet?

MATTHEW BARKER: Everyone knows.

PAUL BARKER: Who was it?

MATTHEW BARKER: Steve Allison.

KIMBERLEY BARKER: Who does everyone think they were talking about?

MATTHEW BARKER: Come on, Mom. Don't play dumb. Don't pretend like this hadn't gone round every Riley parent by about ten o'clock yesterday morning. Or that it's a coincidence that you decided we were having a family dinner tonight.

KIMBERLEY BARKER: I'm sorry.

PAUL BARKER: We heard something from Lauren's mom. You should know she was sick about it.

MATTHEW BARKER: I bet.

KIMBERLEY BARKER: Why did Steve Allison say that? It's such a disgusting thing to do.

MATTHEW BARKER: He's an asshole. Lauren dumped him and he didn't know that she and I were friends, so he's decided I'm somehow to blame for this. It's nothing more sophisticated than that.

KIMBERLEY BARKER: I hate the thought of people talking about you.

MATTHEW BARKER: It's fine. Nobody worth giving a shit about believes them.

PAUL BARKER: That's good.

MATTHEW BARKER: It feels like you want to ask me something.

KIMBERLEY BARKER: What?

MATTHEW BARKER: You're both looking at me like I'm the kid from *The Omen* or something. So just ask me if I know anything about what happened to Lauren.

PAUL BARKER: We didn't say that.

KIMBERLEY BARKER: Do you?

PAUL BARKER: *Kim.*

KIMBERLEY BARKER: I'm sorry, but he's right. I just need to hear him say it.

MATTHEW BARKER: Wow. I was sort of kidding, but OK.

PAUL BARKER: Matt.

KIMBERLEY BARKER: I'm sorry.

MATTHEW BARKER: I don't know what happened to Lauren. I've told the police everything, which isn't much.

KIMBERLEY BARKER: We honestly never thought anything else.

PAUL BARKER: Really.

KIMBERLEY BARKER: I just hope they find her soon.

MATTHEW BARKER: Me too.

PAUL BARKER: You must be worried about her.

MATTHEW BARKER: I am. But I think they'll find her. I think it's going to be OK.

KIMBERLEY BARKER: Me too.

PAUL BARKER: We really didn't think anything, Son. We just had to ask. I'm sorry.

MATTHEW BARKER: It's fine. Can we get back to our totally-not-awkward family dinner now?

Recording ends: March 28, 19:27

March 28th
Journal entry 22

So that was **fun**. A really nice, easy-going family dinner where everyone talks about their days and everyone is happy and your parents ask you if you had anything to do with your friend going missing.

Seriously.

I suppose I get that they felt like they had to do something proactive, so that if anyone talks shit about me they can defend me because they asked me outright and I said no and they believe me.

But still.

You would have thought they could have just assumed that I didn't kidnap my fucking friend, or murder her, or whatever has actually happened to her. I mean, if I *had* kidnapped her, where would I be keeping her? Under my bed? And if I murdered her, when and how? And what would I have done with the body?

I like to hope that they don't think I could do something as awful as any of that to someone, but even if they do, the absence of logic is really infuriating.

School was really weird today. However fast the details of the article in *The Reporter* went around the Riley parents yesterday will have been a fucking snail's pace compared to how fast it went around school.

I was all set to spend a second day defending myself, but that wasn't what happened. I got shitty looks from Steve and his little gang of acolytes, but everyone else was generally pretty cool with me. Elle Solomon and Rachel Kluber both hugged me and told me not to listen to any bullshit, and Andy Lindburgh, who I honestly always thought didn't like me very much, came over at recess and told me his dad would be happy to talk to me if I wanted to sue Steve for what he said.

It seems pretty obvious to me that I can't sue over an article in which I wasn't named and neither were the sources, but I didn't want to seem ungrateful, so I just told him that my parents were both lawyers and had asked friends of theirs to look into it. He looked pleased. I get the feeling he really doesn't like Steve very much, which – obviously – makes me like Andy a lot more than I did.

But yeah. Still weird.

I don't like being the center of attention, for any reason. And for two days now, I definitely have been. But sooner or later there'll be something else for everyone to get all excited about, and right now I feel about as tired as I've ever felt.

So I'm going to bed.

— — — —

March 29th
Journal entry 23

It was 3.14am when I woke up. I guess I shouldn't be surprised.

I was dreaming and it wasn't about Lauren and it wasn't about birds or trees and it wasn't about him and I think I was happy, like I was actually relieved inside the dream, because there was something else inside my head that wasn't dark. Then my phone rang and I tried to answer it but nothing happened, and I think I knew that it was my real phone, actually ringing in the real world, and I think I woke up straight away but I can remember this feeling of disappointment that was so strong it was almost painful, like I knew that this was the end of something and the dream was going to fade away around me.

My eyes opened and I picked up my phone and there was nothing on the screen. Not just no number, but no NUMBER WITHHELD or PRIVATE NUMBER or anything. Just the noise coming out of its speakers and the little red and green circles.

I answered it and held it to my ear and for a long moment there was nothing. Then I heard something in the distance, like a rustling sound, and something else underneath. I listened and I listened and then I understood, and once I did I could hear clearly.

Wind moving through the branches of trees.

Water lapping at the edge of a lake.

I listened for a long time. I don't know how long. There was something comforting about the sounds, like they were coming from a place I knew, a place where I felt at home. It was peaceful.

Then a voice whispered in my ear and I dropped the phone because I clamped both my hands over my mouth so I didn't scream.

By the time I had calmed down enough to pick the phone back up, the line was dead. No more sounds of wind and water, and no more voice.

But I heard it. And I knew who it belonged to. She only said two words, but I heard them both clearly.

Help me.

— — — —

March 29th

Journal entry 24

It's just after four in the morning now.

It's time.

— — — —

TRANSCRIPTS OF AUDIO RECORDED ON MATTHEW BARKER'S CELLPHONE

Recording begins: March 29, 04:22

I don't know if you'll hear this, Ryan. I hope you do, because that will mean it worked, that I went in there and I came back out and I got to send you this and you can tell me what it means.

If you don't, well. I don't know. You'll never know I recorded it I guess, unless someone finds my phone and finds this recording and gets into my email and works out that it's you I'm talking to. I guess that could happen. Maybe. I don't know.

It's cold out here. My phone's in my pocket and I've got my headphones in so I can talk and people will think I'm on a call with someone and not that I'm crazy. There are enough people in this city that just walk around talking to themselves that I'm not sure anyone would even look at me twice, but I guess I don't want to take the risk. New York isn't like it used to be, but it's probably still not the best idea to be walking around looking like a crazy person at four-thirty in the morning.

Anyway. Like I said, it's cold. Nobody heard me leave the apartment. I just walked out the door and pulled it shut gently behind me, and I thought about Lauren doing the same thing, going to wherever she was going. I wonder what was going through her mind that night. Did he call to her? Had she been dreaming about him, like I have? Or did she just know that there was something she had to do, somewhere she was supposed to go. Or maybe she never woke up at all, until she was somewhere else. I'd like to ask her.

Everything looks normal out here. It's never quiet. To be honest, that would be really weird. I can see Central Park West up ahead, and I can see the cars going north toward Harlem. It's all glowing orange under the streetlights and I can see the buildings on the other side of the park above the trees, all the apartment buildings and hotels. There are lights in some of the windows, even now. I guess some people haven't gone to bed yet, and I guess some people are already awake. My dad told me once that his best friend, this guy I've always known as Uncle Dave, used to set his alarm for four AM. I don't know why anyone would do that. There's nothing good that comes from being awake at this hour.

There are people out here too. I just passed a group of guys who were staggering back toward the river, pretty much carrying one of them between the others. They were singing. I kept my head down. I think one of them shouted something at me, but it sounded friendly enough, like the kind of shit drunk people shout at strangers when they're in a good mood, so I just sort of nodded and kept walking and he didn't shout anything else.

OK. I'm crossing Central Park West. There's an entrance to the park a block to the north, where it would probably be easier to climb over, but there's a little turnoff there where cops sometimes park, so that's out. There's only a low brick wall at the edge of the sidewalk here. There's a bigger fence further in, but between the two is trees and shadows and there's much less chance of anyone seeing me go in.

I'm walking north now. There are people coming past me, and I'm walking slowly because I'm waiting for the right moment to go, when nobody is going to be looking right at me. I don't think anyone will give a shit if they see me, unless they're an off-duty cop or something, but still. I'd rather not have some nosey asshole ask me what I'm doing or tell me that the park is closed, like I can't see that for myself.

All right.

There. I'm over. And if anyone saw me, they didn't say anything, so it's all good. I tried to hop over the wall as casually as I could, because I was thinking about not drawing attention to myself but then I realized how stupid that is, because I don't think it matters anymore. So I just stepped up onto the wall and dropped down and I landed on a steep little slope and almost rolled my ankle, but I sort of jumped off of it and landed on the flat and I've just put all my weight on it and it seems like it's OK. It's only going to take me ten minutes to get to the reservoir, so it's only got to hold me up that long.

I wish you were here, man. I know we've never met, and I don't even know if Ryan is really your name and I guess I don't even know whether or not you're really with me on all this shit, or whether you're just humoring me, but you're the only person I can talk to about all this shit that's been invading my head. And so I wish you were here, because this would be easier if I wasn't alone. I think it would be easier. But maybe that's the point, right? That none of this is meant to be easy, that the things that are hard are the things that matter. Shit, I'm rambling.

But it helps to talk this shit through out loud. And talking keeps me warm.

I'm at the fence. It's not all that high, and it's flat on the top, so I don't know why the cops or the park service or whoever think it would ever keep anyone out. I mean, it's high enough that if I overbalance on the way over and land on my head it'll crack wide open, but I don't think that will happen. I don't think he'll let that happen. Because he's been calling me. I'm sure of that now. I didn't know for a while, and then I didn't want to know because I'm a coward and I'm scared, but I can't deny it. The dreams. The fucking birds. The blue light in all the dark. All those pages I never wrote. It's so clear, once you know how to look at it. Once you teach yourself how to see.

OK. I'm over. I did sort of slip on the top, because I had one leg either side and for a second I was balancing on my balls and it was really fucking painful so I sort of had to throw myself over and hope that my legs would swing down before I hit the ground. But they did. My ankle screamed at me again, but I can still walk on it so that's OK for now.

It's dark now. I ran across the main path by Strawberry Fields because it's lit up and I figured that if anyone is going to catch me before I get where I'm going it would be then. But nothing moved, and nobody shouted, and I didn't hear the sound of an engine, so I guess I made it. I'm in the trees now, and I'm heading north. I should reach the edge of the reservoir in five minutes or so. It would be less, but I'm taking it slow. I don't want to make more noise than I have to, and I'm trying to make sure I don't accidentally walk over some sleeping homeless dude. Because I'm not sure that wouldn't be more dangerous than whatever is waiting for me by the water.

That was a joke. Sorry.

Anyway. I've been thinking about all this. About everything that's happened since Lauren went missing, and there's still a little bit of my brain that is sort of looking at myself from the outside, watching me creeping through Central Park in the middle of the night, and wants to know what the fuck I'm thinking. And I get it. Because it's irrational to be doing this, to have gone this far down this path. But it's only a small part now, and the rest of my head hurts, it hurts like someone has put a vice over my ears and tightened it, and I know this is crazy and I know this makes no sense but it's also the only thing that makes any sense at all. Because there are things that you have to accept when there's no other explanation. It's like how you can't see the signal going into your cellphone but you know it's there. You have to accept it, even though you don't really understand. And I didn't write those pages, and I didn't imagine those dreams, and I didn't kill those birds. And I didn't imagine Lauren's voice on my phone. I didn't imagine her asking me to help her. And I don't know, man. I think that maybe there are deep things, things that you can't explain with science, that you can't make sense of when the lights are on and you're warm and safe. I think there are wild things in the dark.

Fuck. I can't breathe. I just
I can't

Recording ends: March 29, 04:31

OK. I'm OK. I had to stop for a second, and as soon as I was stood still I started crying. Properly crying, like I haven't done since I was a little kid.

I don't know. I don't know.

I'm still going north. Or north-east. I think. I don't think I've been in this bit of the park before, but I don't think it matters. I think I'm going to end up in the same place whatever. Because I think that's where I'm supposed to go.

It's darker now. The trees have closed in over the top of me and I can't see the sky anymore. It's OK, I think.

I haven't seen a light for a long time. Or a path. It's all grass and dirt under my feet, and the trees look old. There are no signs now. It doesn't feel like I'm the park anymore. It feels like I'm somewhere else.

I'm going to use my phone as a flashlight. It's so dark. I can't see my hand in front of my face anymore.

It's really quiet. Like I'm the only thing that's alive in here. Like everything else is old and dead and dark.

Jesus. I don't know if I can do this.

I'm really scared.

Recording begins: March 29, 04:49

I tried to go back. I'm sorry, I'm so sorry, but I had to. I can't be here anymore. This is all wrong, this is fucked, this is so bad.

I turned back but there was nothing there. Just darkness. I can't see the sky but I should be able to still see the lights from the buildings but they're not there. It's like they're gone. I went back and I was shining my phone on the ground but my footprints aren't there and I don't know which way is which and I got all turned around and I thought I was going to scream but I bit my lip until I could taste blood in my mouth. I can taste it now. There's no way out and there are just trees in every direction and it's cold and it's dark and I don't know I just don't know I think I fucked up, I think I've fucked up so badly.

Oh God. Oh God.

I don't want this anymore.

I don't

Recording ends: March 29, 04:51

Recording begins: March 29, 04:56

There's something here with me. I can't see it – him – it – I don't know – but I know it's there because I just know, the way some things just are, the way you know things inside your bones and inside your blood. I can hear it moving. It doesn't snap branches and it's feet make no sound, but I can still hear it. I can hear the air moving around it. I can hear it existing. I want to laugh. I don't know why, because nothing's funny but I feel like if I don't laugh I'm going to start screaming and I don't think I'll ever be able to stop. Because it's watching me. I can feel it. It comes so close that I think I could reach out and touch it and part of me wants to because I think that would be the end, that something would sink into me that can't be scrubbed out and there would be black where there's red and then I don't think I would be scared anymore.

I shone my phone around, but it's too quick. Or maybe it's not quick at all. Maybe it just knows how not to be where I point my light. Because I see trees and I see pitch darkness, the color of black holes, the color of emptiness, and I see branches and some of them are really thin and some of them look like they're moving but there's no wind here, not anymore, but by the time I look closely they've stopped or they're gone or I don't have the right kind of eyes.

It's with me. I'm still walking because there's nothing else to do. There's no way out. And I know I fucked up, and I know I made a mistake and I know I deserve this, but I don't want it. I want to go home.

I want to go home.

It's walking with me. I can't even tell anymore if it's going to hurt me. I can't see it but I can feel it and it feels like curiosity, like it wants to watch me like the way you watch a mouse in a maze and it can feel that I'm scared and I think it likes it but I don't know if it actually thinks or feels, like whether I'm trying to process it as human when that's just a fucking stupid waste of time. Stupid. Stupid.

Fucking stupid fucking cry-baby fucking coward.

Christ. Oh please. Please.

Recording ends: March 29, 04:58

Recording begins: March 29, 05:03

I can see light up ahead. It's pale blue and it's glowing and I'm walking toward it because I know that's what it wants me to do but I don't think it's Lauren anymore.

I think maybe it never was.

I think
Oh God
I think
I can see

Recording ends: March 29, 05:05

APRIL 8TH 2018, 20TH POLICE PRECINCT STATION-HOUSE, MANHATTAN, NY

Participants:
Detective John Staglione
Detective Mia Ramirez
Brett Masterson

DET. STAGLIONE.   Can we ask you about that morning? March the 29th.

BRETT MASTERSON.   I told everything I know when I reported it.

DET. RAMIREZ.   We know. We've read your statement. We'd just like to go over it again.

BRETT MASTERSON.   OK. Fine.

DET. STAGLIONE.   You live on East 94th Street?

BRETT MASTERSON.   That's right.

DET. RAMIREZ.   What do you do for a living?

BRETT MASTERSON.   How is that relevant?

DET. STAGLIONE.   This will take longer if you answer our questions with questions.

DET. RAMIREZ.   You work on Wall Street, right?

BRETT MASTERSON.   I do. For the Avery Fund.

DET. RAMIREZ.   Do you run in the park every morning?

BRETT MASTERSON.   When I'm in town.

DET. STAGLIONE.   What time?

BRETT MASTERSON.   I'm usually outside the gates when they open them.

DET. STAGLIONE.   What time is that?

BRETT MASTERSON.   Six.

DET. RAMIREZ.   So you're pretty much the first person in there.

BRETT MASTERSON.   Most mornings there are a few of us.

DET. STAGLIONE.   Waiting to get in?

BRETT MASTERSON.   Right.

DET. RAMIREZ.   You run round the reservoir?

BRETT MASTERSON.   Usually.

DET. STAGLIONE.   So the morning in question. You were there when the gates opened?

BRETT MASTERSON.   Yeah.

DET. RAMIREZ.   And what happened?

BRETT MASTERSON.   I ran.

DET. STAGLIONE.   And then?

BRETT MASTERSON.   I ran round the north side of the lake and I was heading back along the south when I saw someone lying on one of the benches.

DET. RAMIREZ.   Was that unusual?

BRETT MASTERSON.   It didn't used to be. But these days? Yeah.

DET. STAGLIONE.   What did you think when you saw them?

BRETT MASTERSON.   I assumed it was a homeless guy.

DET. RAMIREZ.   So what made you stop?

BRETT MASTERSON.   I got closer and I looked at him as I ran past. I had my headphones on, and I was concentrating on my pace, so it was just a glance, you know? He was asleep, but there was something about him.

DET. STAGLIONE.   What?

BRETT MASTERSON.   He looked clean. I mean, not totally, because his shoes were muddy. Well, his shoe was muddy. He was only wearing one. And so were his jeans, but he was wearing a sweater from Brooks Brothers and his hair looked like it had been washed in the last few days. So I stopped, and I took a closer look, and I saw that he was young. Like, probably twenty at the most. So my first thought was that he had got drunk and climbed the fence and fallen asleep. So I figured I should wake him up.

DET. RAMIREZ.   And you did?

BRETT MASTERSON.   Yeah. I shook his shoulder and he woke up.

DET. STAGLIONE.   What did he say to you?

*   *   *   *

March 29th
Journal entry 25

I think I screamed when the guy woke me up.

I'm not sure, because everything inside my head is heavy, like there's a black hole at the center of it. The guy definitely leapt back, and I think he almost just ran away, but I must have looked so awful when I sat up that he came and sat down next to me. He looked cautious, like he was scared I was going to bite him or something, but I was so pleased that I was still alive and I knew where I was that he was honestly in far more danger of me hugging him and crying on his shoulder.

I told him I was fine. Which was one of the all-time greatest lies I've ever told. But it looked like he believed me. He gave me his business card – seriously, who takes business cards with them when they go for a run? – and asked me if I wanted him to call anyone. I told him where I live, and he didn't look totally convinced, but when I got up to go he didn't try to stop me. I sort of staggered, and my legs didn't feel all that great, but I managed to stay upright and I walked home.

I've honestly never loved the city more than I did during those ten minutes. Every single little bit of – every sound and smell and sight – pumped something that felt weirdly close to joy into my heart and started to warm my bones. I nearly cried when I got to the Central Park West gate and saw a cab drive past. It was mud-splattered yellow and it was going way too fast and there was some fucking terrible music banging out of its open windows but it was just so utterly, amazingly New York that I almost wept.

I can't remember anything after I climbed over the fence. I know I had my phone recording, and I looked at it after I got out of the shower and I saw that I recorded almost forty minutes but I don't know what I said or what's on there because I'm too scared to listen to them. I didn't delete them, but I didn't press play either. I don't know if I ever will. Not any time soon, I'm sure of that.

It's weird. Sometimes when you can't remember something there's almost a shape in your head, like you can see the outline of what's missing, you can almost feel the edges of it. This isn't like that. There's just nothing. A hole where last night should be, so deep that I'm scared to even go near the sides in case I fall in.

I was shaking when I slipped back into the apartment. I don't know if it was the cold or something else. Everything was silent in the apartment, and I heard my dad's alarm go off as I was getting undressed in my room, so I don't think anyone knows I went anywhere. That's good, at least.

I don't know what I was thinking. And all I can think about now is how lucky I am. It feels like some kind of madness descended over me, like everything that makes me a functional human being, one that is at least moderately intelligent and arguably too sensible, just got wiped aside, like some wave of mania crashed into me and made me someone else for a while.

I could have been murdered in the park. Beaten up. Raped. It's safer than it used to be, probably safer than it's ever been, but there's never anywhere that's totally safe to sleep outside when you're in the grip of something and you don't have any way to defend yourself. There's this thing we get taught at school, where we're supposed to just accept as a fact that people are inherently decent, that everyone has their own struggles on their own journey and that everyone deserves the benefit of the doubt.

It's total bullshit, obviously. Some people are just awful. Plenty of them, in all honesty.

So yeah. I know I was lucky.

Really lucky.

I stripped off to get in the shower and my stomach kind of turned because there are scratches and cuts all over me. They aren't bad, but they were a surprise because until I saw them, until I knew they were there, they didn't hurt. They look like the kind of cuts and scratches you end up with if you've been running around a park in the dark all night.

And that was when I realized how tired I really was, because everything started to swim before my eyes. The lines of red looked like they were moving, like they were sliding and twisting into patterns of whirls and loops, and I saw grey at the edges of my vision and I thought I was going to faint.

I squeezed my eyes shut until the feeling passed, and when I opened them again the cuts and scratches were just cuts and scratches. They're not even deep, thankfully. There was a little bit of blood that came off me when I was stood in the shower, but it was barely more than a little streak of pink that disappeared down the plughole.

I wish I could have gone back to bed, but I couldn't face the thought of trying to persuade my parents that I'm ill, so instead I drank two cups of coffee and I stole one of the antidepressants my mom got prescribed after what happened to Brad which are basically pure amphetamine and I feel a bit better. I'm going to crash hard this afternoon, I know that for an absolute fact, but as long as I can make it until school lets out I should be OK.

Nine hours and ten minutes until I can crawl into bed and grab three hours sleep before Mom and Dad get home. Five hundred and fifty minutes and counting.

It'll be fine. *I'll* be fine.

I'm sure I will.

— — — —

Andy Lindburgh

OK. So I'm at school already and one
of the cops is back. And Dr. Phillips just told
me there's a special assembly as soon as
everyone gets in.   08:02

José Sanchez

Shit. That doesn't sound good.   08:04

Steve Allison

What did Phillips say? Exactly?   08:05

Andy Lindburgh

That there's a special assembly
as soon as everyone gets in.
Like I said.   08:05

Elle Solomon

Oh God. I just called Lauren's
apartment and nobody answered.   08:06

Steve Allison

Nobody's answering in the school
office.   08:10

Elle Solomon

Jesus. I can't even.   08:10

Send message

Amy Linares

All of you need to stop assuming the worst. Right now.   08:11

Andy Lindburgh

Amy's right. This might not be that.   08:11

José Sanchez

What else could it be?   08:12

Send message

KIM

Did you hear?

PAUL

Ted Allen just called me. I can't believe it.

KIM

I talked to Amanda's sister. It's definitely her.

PAUL

My God. Have you told Matt?

KIM

He'd left when I heard. I was going to text him but I assume he'll know soon enough.

PAUL

Yeah. I guess he will.

Message   Send

March 29th

HOLY FUCKING SHIT

Elle Solomon

My mom just talked to Lauren's
mom. She's really OK.   10:31

José Sanchez

Thank God for that. Do they know
where she's been?   10:31

Elle Solomon

Her mom said she walked into
their building last night. Their doorman
recognized her and called their
apartment.   10:32

Elle Solomon

Apparently she doesn't remember
anything. She can't tell them where she's
been. But she's alive. And she's safe.
That's all that matters.   10:33

Amy Linares

How's her mom doing?   10:33

Elle Solomon

Mom said she's OK. She's at the
hospital with Lauren's dad. They're
checking her over but they don't think
there's anything wrong with her.   10:34

Send message

Jamie Reynolds
It's crazy. She's back and
she's OK. It's great.   10:34

Andy Lindburgh
Yeah. It's amazing. Am sort of desperate
to know where she's been, though.   10:34

José Sanchez
Me too.   10:35

Elle Solomon
I'm sure she'll tell us when she's
ready. If she can remember.   10:35

Amy Linares
I just want to go and see her.   10:35

Elle Solomon
Me too. Mom said they'll let us know
when she can have visitors.   10:36

Send message

March 29th
Journal entry 27

This is crazy.
It's absolutely crazy.
I can't even get my head around it.

She's back.

I went out last night.
Into the darkness.
And she came back this morning.

Is it a coincidence? I mean, the rational part of my brain is trying to tell me that it is, that it has to be, that that's the only thing it can be.

But that's not what I believe. It's not what I *feel*.

Because something happened last night. I know it did, even though I can't remember. There are things inside that black hole, and it doesn't matter that I can't see them. I went into the park and I did something even though I don't know what and now she's back.

It can't be a coincidence.
It just can't be.

I'm shaking while I type this.

Lauren is back.

Everyone was buzzing by the time I got to Riley this morning. There was already a row of news vans outside and I saw Detective Ramirez talking to a couple of teachers so I knew this was probably going to be it one way or the other. The only thing that remained to be seen was whether or not they'd found Lauren alive or found a corpse.

Lots of the girls were crying, which could have honestly meant anything. A couple of reporters were leaning through the bars on the fence, asking anyone and everyone if they knew what was going on, if they'd heard anything, and teachers and security guards were almost physically pushing their faces back through the bars. It was crazy. The reporters just backed away for a couple of seconds then tried again, trying to tempt kids over, almost *begging* them to talk to them.

Eventually, Dr. Heighway came out and called everyone into the gym. Detective Ramirez was there, along with pretty much the entire faculty, and it was still impossible to know what they were about to tell us. Eventually everyone quieted down and the principal got up on a little podium and said that he was delighted to be able to tell us all that Lauren Bailey had been found alive and well.

People cheered. They actually cheered.

Everyone was instantly on their feet, clapping and screaming, and pretty much everyone immediately had their phone out and were taking photos. Within about five minutes everyone was using #HappyEnding as the hashtag.

Detective Ramirez got up and told us that there was a lot they still didn't know, and a lot she couldn't tell us, but that Lauren had been taken to Mount Sinai for assessment, where she was in good health and talking to her family and the doctors. Somebody shouted out, "Where has she been?" but Ramirez just shook her head and told us that she would keep us all updated as the situation progressed.

Then Dr. Heighway asked everyone for a moment of silence, in which we should all think about how the news made us feel and take a moment to be grateful and happy for her friends and family.

Because she's back and she's alive and she's safe and I know it's because of me, even if I can't ever tell anyone that.

I rescued her.
From him.
Like I knew I had to. Like I said I would.

Jesus.
This is crazy.
So fucking crazy.

I need to talk to her. I need to know where she's been, and if she remembers how she got home.

I need to know if she knows what I did.

And I need to talk to someone.

— — — —

Breaker1989 <breakerbreaker1989 @gmail.com>
To: RightHereRightThere <righthere8rightthere9@gmail.com>
Date: 29 March at 12:36
Subject: Are you there?

Did you see?

RightHereRightThere <righthere8rightthere9@gmail.com>
To: Breaker1989 <breakerbreaker1989 @gmail.com>
Date: 29 March at 12:38
Subject: RE: Are you there?

Jesus, Matt. I've just read about it. This is totally nuts.

What did you do? What the fuck happened last night?

Breaker1989 <breakerbreaker1989 @gmail.com>
To: RightHereRightThere <righthere8rightthere9@gmail.com>
Date: 29 March at 12:38
Subject: RE: Are you there?

I don't know.

RightHereRightThere <righthere8rightthere9@gmail.com>
To: Breaker1989 <breakerbreaker1989 @gmail.com>
Date: 29 March at 12:38
Subject: RE: Are you there?

What do you mean?

Breaker1989 <breakerbreaker1989 @gmail.com>
To: RightHereRightThere <righthere8rightthere9@gmail.com>
Date: 29 March at 12:39
Subject: RE: Are you there?

I went into the park. I can't remember anything. And then this morning she was back.

RightHereRightThere <righthere8rightthere9@gmail.com>
To: Breaker1989 <breakerbreaker1989 @gmail.com>
Date: 29 March at 12:40
Subject: RE: Are you there?

Fuuuuuuuuuck. This is crazy.

She's really back? I read about it at the FUCKING NEW YORK TIMES so I'm guessing there's no way someone has got this wrong?

Breaker1989 <breakerbreaker1989 @gmail.com>
To: RightHereRightThere <righthere8rightthere9@gmail.com>
Date: 29 March at 12:41
Subject: RE: Are you there?

I haven't seen her. But they told everyone at my school today. The cops were there. They're certain it's her.

RightHereRightThere <righthere8rightthere9@gmail.com>
To: Breaker1989 <breakerbreaker1989 @gmail.com>
Date: 29 March at 12:41
Subject: RE: Are you there?

Where has she been?

Breaker1989 <breakerbreaker1989 @gmail.com>
To: RightHereRightThere <righthere8rightthere9@gmail.
com>
Date: 29 March at 12:42
Subject: RE: Are you there?

They're not saying. Some people were saying she can't
remember.

RightHereRightThere <righthere8rightthere9@gmail.com>
To: Breaker1989 <breakerbreaker1989 @gmail.com>
Date: 29 March at 12:43
Subject: RE: Are you there?

This is the most amazing thing I've ever heard.

You know you did this, right? I mean, you get that? Tell me you
get that?

Breaker1989 <breakerbreaker1989 @gmail.com>
To: RightHereRightThere <righthere8rightthere9@gmail.
com>
Date: 29 March at 12:44
Subject: RE: Are you there?

I don't know what I did. I need you to listen to something for me.

RightHereRightThere <righthere8rightthere9@gmail.com>

To: Breaker1989 <breakerbreaker1989 @gmail.com>

Date: 29 March at 12:44

Subject: RE: Are you there?

What?

Breaker1989 <breakerbreaker1989 @gmail.com>

To: RightHereRightThere <righthere8rightthere9@gmail. com>

Date: 29 March at 12:45

Subject: RE: Are you there?

I don't know. I recorded it last night, while I was in the park. I'm too scared to listen to it myself.

RightHereRightThere <righthere8rightthere9@gmail.com>

To: Breaker1989 <breakerbreaker1989 @gmail.com>

Date: 29 March at 12:45

Subject: RE: Are you there?

Send it.

Breaker1989 <breakerbreaker1989 @gmail.com>

To: RightHereRightThere <righthere8rightthere9@gmail. com>

Date: 29 March at 12:46

Subject: RE: Are you there?

Attached.

RightHereRightThere <righthere8rightthere9@gmail.com>
To: Breaker1989 <breakerbreaker1989 @gmail.com>
Date: 29 March at 13:22
Subject: RE: Are you there?

___

Dude. That is incredible. Did you really record that last night?

Breaker1989 <breakerbreaker1989 @gmail.com>
To: RightHereRightThere <righthere8rightthere9@gmail.com>
Date: 29 March at 13:23
Subject: RE: Are you there?

___

Yeah. Should I listen to it?

RightHereRightThere <righthere8rightthere9@gmail.com>
To: Breaker1989 <breakerbreaker1989 @gmail.com>
Date: 29 March at 13:23
Subject: RE: Are you there?

___

You definitely need to listen to it. Straight away.

I can't believe this. I just can't. You literally went into the darkness and brought her out. I mean, I don't even know what the consequences are going to be, but you did it. You brought her back.

You're a fucking hero. Seriously.

Breaker1989 <breakerbreaker1989 @gmail.com>
To: RightHereRightThere <righthere8rightthere9@gmail.com>
Date: 29 March at 13:24
Subject: RE: Are you there?

She was my friend, and I knew I had to do something. I just couldn't leave her out there on her own.

I wish I could remember last night. Maybe I'll listen to the recordings, if I feel up to it.

But whatever happened, I couldn't have done it without you. Thank you for believing me.

RightHereRightThere <righthere8rightthere9@gmail.com>
To: Breaker1989 <breakerbreaker1989 @gmail.com>
Date: 29 March at 13:26
Subject: RE: Are you there?

You are more than welcome, dude.

March 30 2018. NEW YORK.

MISSING TEENAGER "FOUND ALIVE AND WELL"

by Nicole Sheridan

Lauren Bailey, the daughter of prominent gynecologist Dr. Lawrence Bailey, is being treated in Mount Sinai Hospital after going missing for more than a week.

Students at the Riley School, where Lauren is an Honor Roll senior, were told yesterday morning by school staff and NYPD Detectives who have been investigating the pretty blonde's disappearance, that she had been found "alive and well."

No further details have been officially provided, but sources close to the Bailey family said that Lauren walked back into her family's building on the Upper East Side in the early hours of yesterday morning, where she was immediately recognized by a doorman who called the Bailey's apartment. Lauren's mother, Amanda Bailey, contacted police and traveled with her daughter to Mount Sinai, where sources have described her as alert and in good health.

No explanation for her disappearance has yet been given, and it may be some time until the mystery is cleared up, if ever. My sources at the Riley School have told me that Lauren Bailey apparently has no memory of the past week, and has been unable to provide authorities with any details of her whereabouts or whether any other persons were involved.

Reached for comment at her desk at the 20th Precinct, NYPD Detective Mia Ramirez, who has been leading the team investigating Lauren's disappearance, would say only that she was "delighted that Lauren had been found, and that her parents have their daughter back safe and sound."

Thousands of hours of police time have been dedicated to the search for Lauren Bailey. Policing experts have claimed that the investigation will have cost New York taxpayers tens of thousands of dollars.

Dr. Lawrence Bailey, who this column exclusively revealed has been staying at a hotel in recent days, and who has been the subject of widespread accusations of high-profile infidelity, was seen entering Mount Sinai Hospital in the early hours of yesterday morning. His clinic on Madison Avenue remains closed, and calls to both the clinic's switchboard and Dr. Bailey's out-of-hours number continue to go unanswered.

TRANSCRIPTS OF AUDIO RECORDED ON MATTHEW BARKER'S CELLPHONE

Recording begins: March 30, 03:17

Ah. Ah. Jesus. Ah fucking Jesus Christ. Jesus.

I thought I was done with this.

Seriously.

I can't.
I just can't.

I know I'm awake now and I now I was dreaming then. I know it this time. Because there was nothing normal, nothing even close to normal about that. That was fucked.

Jesus. My heart's going to burst out of my chest.

Hold on.

Recording ends: March 30, 03:18

Recording begins: March 30, 03:20

OK. I've got a glass of water and all the lights in my bedroom are on and I'm trying really hard not to cry because I thought yesterday was the end of all this. Like, what more am I supposed to do. I went into the dark and there's a hole in my mind with fucking poison leaking out of it but Lauren's back and she's safe and that was the trade, right? I went in there and I faced whatever it is and it doesn't matter if I can't remember it because that doesn't matter. I was scared but I went and I stood and she came back. Fair trade.

FAIR FUCKING TRADE FOR FUCK'S SAKE.

Shit. My heart's fucked. It's fucked. It's going to break my ribs.

I just.
I can't.

Recording ends: March 30, 03:21

Recording begins: March 30, 03:24

I was underwater.

I don't know where, because it was dark, and I couldn't see anything around me. Like I couldn't see the sides of a bathtub or a pool, and I couldn't see weeds or plants or fish or anything else that would have made me think I was in a river or the sea or something. I was just underwater, and it was so cold.

It was freezing. Everything felt like ice, frozen cold and heavy and dead. I was shaking like I was being electrocuted and I was trying to scream but I was scared to open my mouth because I would have swallowed water and I knew I would drown and I had this fear, this absolute fucking terror, that I would drown in the dream and I would die and then I would never wake up, like my mom would come into my room in the morning and find me either dead or brain-dead, like a fuckin' vegetable, and part of my brain was wondering which would be worse but most of it was screaming with panic and the surface was just above me, I could see light, I could see the bubbles breaking on the surface, and I was thrashing but I couldn't move because something was holding me.

Something was holding me under the water.

There were things wrapped around my arms and legs, things that moved and pulsed like snakes. They didn't feel like arms. They felt like fucking snakes, and I know because one of them was round my neck and it was sort of flexing, like it was breathing and moving and tightening itself then loosening itself then tightening itself again, in case I thought even for a second that it might be going to let me go.

They felt like octopus limbs, but without the suckers.

No fuck that. They felt like snakes. That's what they felt like.

Like tentacles.

It felt like my chest was going to burst and I was trying to get the things – the tentacles – off my arms but then I stopped moving, because I knew there was something looking at me. I just knew. And I looked up through the water, and I could see it. Him. I don't know.

This shape, thin and black, with this white oval which I think was its face. It was just above the water, inches away from me, but I couldn't see it clearly, because the water was swirling and full of bubbles and it was getting darker, it was literally getting darker in front of my eyes, and it was just hanging there above me, not moving, just looking down at me. And I realized that the things, the tentacles that were holding me, were part of him. And he was holding me under water and he was going to watch me drown, and I sort of felt this enormous thing, like I was seeing a fraction of something so huge that my mind couldn't really process it, like I was looking up through a keyhole and he was the only thing I could see, was the only thing in the universe, was all there was.

I couldn't keep my mouth close any longer. I fought and fought, but I couldn't. So I opened my mouth, and I breathed in, and dark water poured down my throat and I felt it filling me and I screamed but no sound came out.

And I woke up.

Jesus.

I thought this was over.
I really did.

Recording ends: March 30, 03:28

March 30ᵗʰ
Journal entry 28

There was a moment yesterday when I didn't feel like this.

When we were in the gym and Dr. Heighway told us all that Lauren was back, that she was safe, I felt something so overwhelming that I can't really describe it. I felt happiness, and I felt love for her and her parents and Elle and Rachel and everyone else who has missed her and worried about her, and I felt something else, something deeper. **I felt proud.**

I felt so fucking proud of myself.

Today, I felt like a zombie.

The nightmare was so bad, so far beyond bad, that I felt like less of a person than usual, like something had reached inside me and dragged out a big chunk of what makes me me. Everyone at school was still buzzing about Lauren's return, wondering when she's going to be back at school, still speculating endlessly about where she's been, although with notably less venom than before. People seem like they're more sympathetic now, because the story had a happy ending, because now there's no chance of the gruesome, horror-movie ending that lots of them were secretly hoping for.

I sort of sleepwalked through it all. Last week I would have worried that people would notice my grey skin and the absence of anything even approaching a smile. Because last week at least some of the people I spend most of every day with thought I had something to do with Lauren going missing. But now she's back, and I think I managed to just fade into the background.

I can't remember going to class. I'm pretty sure I did, but there's a black hole where those memories should be. It feels like my brain is too tired and too traumatized to make new memories, like it's somehow become read-only.

I don't know what I did in the park. I still haven't listened to the recording I sent to Ryan.

I can't.

There are flashes in the back of my head, images that feel disassociated from anything else. Darkness, and the rustle of trees. A light that was maybe blue.

I don't know. I want to tell myself that it's all a coincidence, that my brain – that was already tired from months of nightmares – made me do something stupid, something that I should objectively know I was really, really lucky to get away with, and that Lauren coming back the next day was just luck. Just blind, dumb luck, that only an idiot would believe was anything else.

I want to tell myself that. I've tried. I've really, really tried.

But I can't even manage to convince myself.

Because I feel more certain about this than about anything else I've ever known.

It was real.
It happened.
And it isn't over.

I went into the darkness and I went on my own because what's happening is only happening to me and I went into that place and the next morning Lauren was back. And if you'd seen what I've seen, and felt what I've felt, you wouldn't be able to believe it was a coincidence either.

Christ. My mind feels like its creaking. Like it only needs one more gentle push and it's going to snap.

What would that feel like? Would I even know it had happened?

I don't know.

My only hope now – honestly, the only thing I still care about – is that Lauren somehow knows what I did.

But I doubt that.

From what people were saying this morning, it sounds like she's got the same black hole in her head that I have. And to be honest, I'm glad. Because I don't know where she was and I don't know what was happening to her while she was gone, but I find it really, really hard to believe that it was anything that she'll want to remember.

Maybe it will always eat at her, like an itch you can't scratch. Maybe she'll want more than anything to remember, and maybe it will destroy her that she can't. But I think I'll always believe she's better off.

Some things can't be recovered from. Some things persist. Some things won't ever let you go.

And that's the truth at the heart of this, the truth that I'm almost too scared to admit to myself.

This story isn't finished.

And I don't know if it ever will be.

— — — —

JAMIE

What have you heard about Lauren?

MATT

What are you talking about?

JAMIE

People are saying things. Somebody said
she had remembered where she was,
someone else said they were letting her
go home. Wondered if you'd heard anything.

MATT

I haven't heard anything.

JAMIE

Would you tell me if you had?

MATT

Yes.

JAMIE

OK. I guess I'll believe that.

JAMIE

Are you all right?

MATT

What are you talking about?

JAMIE

You looked like shit today.

MATT

Thanks.

📷 Message   Send

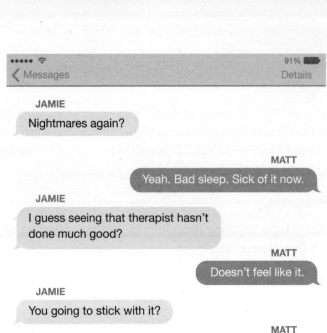

JAMIE
Nightmares again?

MATT
Yeah. Bad sleep. Sick of it now.

JAMIE
I guess seeing that therapist hasn't done much good?

MATT
Doesn't feel like it.

JAMIE
You going to stick with it?

MATT
I don't really have a choice.

JAMIE
I guess not.

JAMIE
Let me know if you hear anything about Lauren. Everyone is kind of freaking out waiting for news.

MATT
OK.

MATT
I'm getting called for dinner. Speak to you later.

JAMIE
See you.

📷   Message   Send

March 30th

Journal entry 29

Don't email Ryan. Don't email Ryan. Don't email Ryan. Don't email Ryan. Don't email Ryan. Don't email Ryan. Don't email Ryan. Don't email Ryan. Don't email Ryan. Don't email Ryan. Don't email Ryan. Don't email Ryan. Don't email Ryan. Don't email Ryan.

Seriously.

You don't know anything about him. He was cool, but then he wasn't. Don't forget that.

You don't know if he really believes you.

And even if he does, there's nothing he can do.

He can't help.

Nobody can.

— — — —

TRANSCRIPTS OF AUDIO RECORDED ON MATTHEW BARKER'S CELLPHONE

Recording begins: March 31, 03:42

I don't know how nobody else woke up. I really don't. Because it sounded like a fucking machine gun going off.

I thought my heart was going to burst when I woke up, it was so loud. And I wasn't dreaming, and that was amazing, and then there was just this huge fucking rattle, like someone was beating the entire apartment with a hammer or something.

I feel OK now, though. And that makes me feel weird, because nothing is OK, what I just cleared up wasn't even anywhere close to OK, but I'm scared that I'm just getting used to it now. Like my brain doesn't react like it used to when something fucking awful and terrifying happens, and that really scares me, because what if I'm not the same person I used to be? What if something has changed inside me that I don't know how to change back? Because there's all this darkness and there's all this shit that I can't explain and I just sort of accept it and deal with it now, like it isn't even a big deal, and that's fucked.

That's not how normal people behave.

I got up when I heard the noise. I was expecting to run into my dad in the corridor, because I seriously don't know how him and my mom didn't hear it. But the apartment was dark, and I leant up against their bedroom door and I could hear Dad snoring, so I knew I was on my own.

It was dark in the kitchen, and in the lounge. The shadows were deep and I checked every one of them. Every single one. But nothing moved, and everything was still, and I was on my own.

I'm sure I was.

I waited to see if the noise came again, but it didn't. Everything was quiet. There was a thin line of moonlight shining in through the gap between the curtains, and it was like this bright line in the middle of the darkness, like it was pointing at something, or leading somewhere. I was shaking and I'm telling myself now that it was because of the cold but I'm really not sure it was.

I walked over and I pulled back one of the curtains and for a long time I just stared at what was there, because I couldn't move and I don't think I was breathing because my heart was frozen solid in my chest and I'm not even sure I blinked. I just stared and stared and stared.

The door that opens onto the terrace was covered in blood.

It was splashed and smeared all over the glass, running down toward the ground. I reached out, without even realizing I was doing so, and touched a thick smear and I realized that the blood was on the other side and I think that was what sort of unlocked my insides, that made me take this rattling breath that sounded so loud to me that I clamped a hand over my mouth so nobody else heard it.

I didn't know what to do. I couldn't see where the blood had come from. It was just there, glistening and dripping. And part of my brain was screaming at me that it wasn't real, that it couldn't be real, that I should just go back to bed and go back to sleep and in the morning it wouldn't be there because it had never been there, but the bigger part of my brain, the part that is cold now and was looking at the blood like it was barely anything out of the ordinary, told me that there was no point lying to myself.

It was real. I knew it was.

I unlocked the door and slid it open. The air that came in from the outside was cold and I shivered, but I barely felt it. The terrace outside was dark and covered in shadows and my mind was racing, thinking of all the things that could be out there, waiting for me. And I had this thought, like the way that when you're a kid you think there's a monster under your bed but it won't be able to get you as long as you keep your arms and legs under the covers, like there's a logic that's unimpeachable. It was like that.

I was thinking that as long as I stayed inside the apartment, I would be safe. Like it wouldn't be able to come in. He wouldn't be able to come in.

But I had to see. I just had to.

It was less quiet on the terrace. I could hear the cars driving past below, and I could hear distant voices, even at that time in the morning. There wasn't much wind, but the air was cold, and the park was lit with all its usual lights and all the buildings were glowing with yellow and I could see the light reflecting off the water in the reservoir. I checked the corners first. Where it was darkest. But there was nothing. Then I turned round and looked at the window and

I just. Jesus. I wish I could explain how it felt. How it wasn't so much horror, or even fear at all, it was just that it was fucking *wrong*.

There were birds all over the terrace. Maybe thirty of them, maybe more. They were lying in a thick pool of blood and the blood was running down the glass and it was everywhere and I sort of remember thinking that there shouldn't be that much blood birds are only small and how much damage could they have really done themselves by flying into the window but then I went closer and I looked at the mess, at all the blood and the feathers, and I saw why there was so much of it.

The birds looked like they'd been turned inside out.

There was bits of pink and purple, things that weren't supposed to be visible. Things that shouldn't be out. They were shiny and some of them were moving, like there was still life in them, or maybe just that they were still pulsing because until a few minutes ago they were still warm and running with blood and doing whatever they were supposed to be doing inside the birds. It was all shiny and there was this faint little cloud of steam rising from it all and it smelt like meat and puke and I had to stop looking at it because I was going to throw up right on top of it all if I didn't. So I looked at the window. And then I wished I hadn't.

Because from this side, I could see. The blood had splashed and sprayed and run toward the terrace in thick rivers and where it had run together there was a shape on the glass. A tall, thin shape, much taller than me. With arms and things emerging from its back. Things that

Limbs.
Tentacles.

Oh God.

OK. OK.

I couldn't look at it. I thought I was going to go mad if I did, like I was teetering on the edge of a cliff and if I fell I was never going to be able to catch myself. So I went back inside and I shut the door and I started to cry and I tried to tell myself to snap out of it, to just fucking stop it. I slapped myself across the face and I screamed at myself inside my head but the tears wouldn't stop. It was like someone had turned on a tap behind my eyes and snapped it off.

I don't know how long I cried for.

I know what time is it now, and I think I know what time I heard the noise, but that doesn't seem right. It doesn't feel like long enough. It feels like time doesn't matter as much as it used to, like it's stretchier and thinner than I realized, something you can push and pull and twist and tear.

I wanted to wake my parents and crawl into bed between them and have them tell me everything is OK, tell me that there are no monsters in the shadows, that everything is really, truly going to be all right.

When I finally stopped crying I got a trash bag from the kitchen and took it back out onto the terrace. I didn't look at the bloody figure and I didn't look at what used to be the birds. I went to the little shed in the corner where Mom keeps the seeds and plant food and grabbed the little shovel that Dad uses to clear the snow when it comes.

I scooped us as much of the mess as I could manage without really looking at it. The smell got into my nose and I gagged and my eyes were streaming and I could sort of feel it all shifting and moving as I dumped it into the trash bag and I think I got some of it on my hand and then I did puke, straight into the bag onto top of all the feathers and guts. I puked until there was nothing left inside of me.

I got most of it. There was blood in the cracks between the paving stones and there was blood smeared on the metal legs of the table and the chairs, and there was blood all over the window, but the worst of it was gone. I tied off the bag and I grabbed the hosepipe and I turned it on. I wondered for about half a second whether the noise would wake my parents but I didn't care anymore by then, and if the fucking machine gun of the birds smashing into the glass so hard they ripped themselves to pieces then I figured it would probably be OK.

I washed away the awful bloody figure on the glass and I sprayed the red down the drain and I sprayed the furniture and I sprayed the stones. When I was finished there was still spots of red and smears of pink, but I couldn't do anything about them. And as I carried the heavy, warm bag through the apartment and out into the corridor where I dumped it into the trash chute, a voice in the back of my head was telling me not to worry about the blood.

That it didn't matter.

Because nobody else would be able to see it anyway.

Recording ends: March 31, 03:49

Warning. (i.redd.it)(Slender_Man)

submitted 2 hours ago * by gemini15

I've been thinking about u/breakerbreaker1989's posts. Can't stop thinking about them to be honest. And I just want to tell everyone that nothing ever good comes from meddling with things you don't understand. You step into the darkness and you don't get to be surprised by what you find there.

There's no taking it back. There's always a price to be paid. You can't unsee what you've seen.

That's all I want to say. I hope he's OK.
1 comment share save hide give gold report

all 1 comments
sorted by **oldest**

[-] **jkkhh** 0 points 1 hour ago
Try harder.
perma-link embed save report give gold reply

April 1st
Journal entry 30

I'm OK. I'm awake and it's light outside and I feel OK.

I haven't been out onto the terrace. I did what I could last night. There's nothing else I can do about it now.

Now I just have to get through school and somehow get through my appointment with Dr. Casemiro – which is at fucking **lunchtime** today, because obviously her schedule is so much more important than mine – and then I can go back to bed.

Although, to be honest, that's not really something I've looked forward to for a long time.

— — — —

April 1st
Journal entry 31

Dr. Casemiro always looks a little bit disappointed we finish a session.

It's like I just didn't give her what she wanted, that somehow I failed. Part of me thinks that a psychiatrist shouldn't be so easy to read, but most of me doesn't really give a shit. I'm just glad she's gone.

She was the same as she always is, really gentle and polite and acting like she's my friend. She asked me if I was still having the nightmares and I said yes because I thought it would sound too unbelievable if I said no, like they'd just stopped all of a sudden. There's no way she would have bought that. So I told her I was still having them, but I didn't tell her how bad they've gotten and I definitely didn't tell her what they're like now, the things that I've seen. I didn't want to make her any more interested in me.

We talked about other stuff, like we always do. I think she thinks that if she can sort out all the little bits and pieces that are wrong in my life, that are unsatisfactory, then the nightmares will just go away. And maybe that was an option, once. Maybe that's what would have happened.

I know it's too late for that now. But she doesn't need to know that. Nobody else does.

She asked me about school and I told her the truth, that things are really quickly going back to normal. There's this big thing looming on the horizon that everyone is waiting for, which is when Lauren comes back to school and everyone gets to actually see her and talk to her and hug her and tell her how much they missed her. That will be a big day, the kind of day that blows up social media and causes about a billion snaps and WhatsApp messages to be sent. But after that, I think it will be over.

For everyone else, at least. Including Lauren. I hope.

Dr. Casemiro asked me about her, but I sort of dodged the question. She knows that we're friends, and I told her I was worried about her when she was missing and I was relieved when she came back safe. That's all she needs to hear.

The rest is none of her business.

— — — —

Elle Solomon
I just saw Lauren.   13:21

Amy Linares
What?   13:21

José Sanchez
Did they let her out?   13:21

Elle Solomon
She's home. I just left there.   13:21

Amy Linares
Why didn't you tell me?   13:22

Andy Lindburgh
Is she OK? How's she doing?   13:22

Elle Solomon
I didn't know I was going, Amy. My mom called and told me to come home. We went over there.   13:23

Elle Solomon
She's OK. She really doesn't remember where she's been, and that's messing her up badly. But she's all right, I think. She mostly just seemed like Lauren.   13:23

Send message

José Sanchez
That's great.   13:24

Amy Linares
What did the doctors say?   13:24

Elle Solomon
They said she's OK. She was dehydrated
when they took her in, and they don't think
she ate much while she was missing, but
there's nothing physically wrong with her.
They want her to see a psychiatrist.   13:25

Andy Lindburgh
Do they think she'll remember where
she's been?   13:25

Elle Solomon
They don't know. They hope so.   13:25

Amy Linares
But she's OK?   13:26

Elle Solomon
She's OK.   13:26

Send message

April 1st
Journal entry 32

Jesus. I don't even know what just happened. I know I wasn't asleep, and I know that it felt real. But I don't know.

Fuck.

I need to tell someone.

I have to.

— — — —

Breaker1989 <breakerbreaker1989 @gmail.com>
To: RightHereRightThere <righthere8rightthere9@gmail.
com>
Date: 1 April at 17:22
Subject: It just snowed inside my apartment

I need to tell you about what happened when I got home.
I walked home and I managed to dodge all the kids from
school who live in my neighborhood and I got home and
got the elevator and as soon as I turned my key in the door
and pushed it open I knew something was wrong. It wasn't
anything I could see, or hear: the apartment was still, and
it wasn't silent, because it never is. I could hear the fridge
humming and the loose floorboard near the door creaked when
I stepped on it. But I could feel something was wrong.

I could feel that I wasn't alone.

I walked through the kitchen and put my bag down on the
table. Then I breathed out, and I could see my breath in the air.
It was colder than it had been when I opened the door, about
thirty seconds earlier. And it was getting colder. I could feel
the temperature dropping. The hair shot up on my arms, and
I shivered. Because it was suddenly as cold as the inside of a
freezer. So fucking cold.

I looked around, and I was shivering, and I was sure it was
getting darker. Like the sun was setting inside the apartment,
like it was turning to night right in front of my eyes. The
shadows were lengthening, crawling up the walls, spreading
out across the floor. I watched them, and I don't think I was
breathing, because I was so sure they were going to start
moving, going to stretch and lengthen and turn into limbs and
tentacles.

294

Then something floated past my face.

I watched it drift down to the floor, and I closed my eyes for a long time, because I could see what it was and what it was made no sense, absolutely no sense at all.

It was a snowflake.

It landed on the floor, and it melted, leaving a little spot of water on the wood. I stared at it for I don't even know how long. Until another snowflake floated down past me, and another, and another. I looked up and the ceiling of the apartment was right there, exactly the same as it always is. But as I looked, I saw snow appear out of the dark air, like it was passing through a window I couldn't see. It started falling harder and harder, drifting down and settling on the floor. I didn't move, and I didn't do anything. I just stared, because I don't think my brain was working properly. Or at all, maybe. I took a step and the snow crunched under my sneaker and I think I cried out, because it was real. It wasn't just in my head, it wasn't some hallucination, it was snow and it was real and I could feel it beneath my foot.

It started to swirl and fall harder and harder. And then there was a blizzard roaring inside our lounge and I almost laughed, because I honestly didn't know what else to do. It was getting darker and darker and the snow was piling up, so quickly that it had already buried the coffee table and most of the sofas, and I felt this sort of itch on the back of my neck, and I knew something was behind me.

I didn't want to turn around. I really didn't. But I couldn't help it. It was like I had no say in it, like what I wanted was suddenly the least important thing in the world.

So I turned around. Or I got turned around. I don't know. And I saw.

The walls of the apartment were gone. There was just darkness in every direction, and snow swirling down from a sky that wasn't there. The shadows had run together and had pulled themselves up off the ground, like something had twisted them together and lifted them up, and I stared at them and as I stared at them they solidified, like they had been liquid that had suddenly set.

He stood in front of me. It stood in front of me. Him.

Black that sucked in every tiny mote of light. Tall and thin with limbs that moved so slowly I couldn't even be sure I was seeing them move at all. This white space where his face should have been. No eyes, although I could tell it was looking at me. He was looking at me.

No mouth, although I could swear it was smiling.

He was smiling at me.

I wanted to run, Ryan. I wanted to run so badly. But the snow had piled up around my legs and I was so cold, so cold that it felt like my blood was frozen solid, and I tried to tell my feet to move but nothing happened, and when nothing happened I tried to look away but my head wouldn't move either. Nothing moved. Except for him.

He leaned toward me, so slowly that it was like watching the seasons change, it was like watching tectonic plates shift. Thousands of hours. Millennia. With absolutely implacability.

At some point I started to scream. That's the last thing I remember before everything went black. The sound of my own screams.

I woke up on the sofa. The clock said I'd been home for ten minutes, but I felt like I'd been gone for years, like every last tiny flicker of energy had been sucked out of me. The walls were where they should be, the ceilings too. There was no snow, and nothing was wet. The apartment was warm and dry and everything looked normal. And it *felt* normal, too. Like whatever was going to happen had happened.

Like I was on my own again.

That's what happened. And I don't know what it meant, and I don't know if it was real or if there's something broken inside my head now, if something has come loose.

This is where I am.

This is where I live.

RightHereRightThere <righthere8rightthere9@gmail.com>
To: Breaker1989 <breakerbreaker1989 @gmail.com>
Date: 1 April at 17:41
Subject: RE: It just snowed inside my apartment

Good to hear from you, Matt. I hope you won't mind if I tell you I've been worried about you. Sadly, it sounds from your email – which I absolutely believe, just so you know that upfront – that I was right to be.

I'll tell you what I think about this as straight as I can, my friend. I owe you nothing less.

I think you're in terrible danger.

You took something from SM. I don't know how – I don't know if we'll ever know – but you did it, and that was a remarkable, brave, brilliant thing. But there were always going to be consequences to what you did – I think you probably knew that too, if you're completely honest with yourself.

You're seeing those consequences now. And I think we both know that things are going to get worse unless you take action again. I doubt this is what you want to hear, and I don't know whether you have it in you to summon up that kind of courage a second time, but you are where you are, and the clock is ticking now.

If you don't do anything, I think we both know what will happen. I'm not going to type it out, but we know. And I don't know if you can do what you did a second time – it may have been that there was only enough magic in the world for you to manage it once, to go into the darkness and stand and be true and drag someone back into the light.

Maybe it can't be done again. I don't know. But I know this: if anyone can do it, it's you.

Tell me if there's anything I can do to help. And, as ever, don't tell anyone about this, or about us talking like this. I can tell you with absolute certainty that nobody else will understand. But I think you already know that, don't you?

Think clearly, my friend. And be careful.

Ryan

Elle Solomons

Lauren's coming back today.   13:12

José Sanchez

WHAT? Back to school?   13:13

Elle Solomons

Yeah. The doctors cleared her.   13:13

Amy Linares

I talked to her last night. She seemed good.   13:14

Amy Linares

I think she just wants to get back to normal.   13:14

Send message

Participants:
Detective John Staglione
Detective Mia Ramirez
Jamie Reynolds
Donald McArthur (Attorney-at-Law)

DET. STAGLIONE.   How did people react?

JAMIE REYNOLDS.   To what?

DET. RAMIREZ.   To Lauren Bailey being back at school.

JAMIE REYNOLDS.   Everyone was pleased to see her.
Although it was weird. I don't think people knew how to act
around her.

DET. RAMIREZ.   What do you mean?

JAMIE REYNOLDS.   It was like, were we supposed to talk
about her going missing? Or were we supposed to just not
mention it and act like everything was normal?

DET. STAGLIONE.   What did people do?

JAMIE REYNOLDS.   Most people didn't mention it. They
were sort of insanely positive, like she was some delicate
thing that everyone had to be really careful with. So people
were telling her all the gossip, and then you would see
someone say something that had happened while she was
away and catch themselves, like they weren't sure whether
to keep talking or not.

DET. RAMIREZ.   How was Lauren?

JAMIE REYNOLDS.   I didn't talk to her the day she came back. But she seemed OK. I think she knew that she couldn't avoid this huge thing, the biggest thing that had ever happened at Riley, but I think she wished she could. By lunchtime she just looked really tired, and Elle and Amy were sticking close to her, like they were her bodyguards or something.

DET. STAGLIONE.   Did she talk to Matthew Barker?

JAMIE REYNOLDS.   You know she did.

DET. RAMIREZ.   You were there? In the cafeteria?

JAMIE REYNOLDS.   I was there.

DET. RAMIREZ.   What happened?

*   *   *   *

April 2nd
Journal entry 33

She said she dreamed about me.

Then when I asked her if there was water when she was, she looked like she'd seen a ghost.

And I know she was going to say something else before Rachel Kluber appeared next to us and started talking about some fucking nonsense Spanish quiz.

She said she dreamed about me while she was gone.

Holy shit.

I need to know what that means. Because maybe it means I'm not crazy, that I'm not losing my mind. Maybe it means that what happened was real, that I went into some dark place and I found her and I brought her back. I mean, what else could it be? Why else would dreaming about me be the only thing she can remember? And why would she have reacted like she did when I asked her about water?

Jesus.

I want to talk to her. I want to text her but I heard someone asking Elle why Lauren had got a new number and Elle told them that the police asked her not to use the same one because her old phone is still missing and they want to monitor whether anyone uses it, so I can't. I could go over to her apartment and ask to see her but it might look weird, and apparently her parents aren't letting her out of their sight right now, so that's out too.

It goes without saying that I can't talk to my parents about this. And I can't talk to Brad, even though I know he wouldn't laugh at me or make fun of me or try to tell me it's all in my head. Because that's not enough. I don't know if anything ever will be.

And I definitely, definitely can't talk to Dr. Casemiro. I got home about an hour ago and there was a letter in our mail slot in reception. I recognized the handwriting on the address right away and I deliberated for all of about ten seconds before I opened it.

— — — —

From the desk of
DR. JENNIFER CASEMIRO, M.D.
596 WEST 72ND STREET, NY 10021

April 2, 2018

Dear Paul and Kimberley,
I'm writing to let you know that my session with Matthew
yesterday lunchtime (the 1ˢᵗ) raised some concerns that I
feel I should share with you.

As I have noted before, and as you told me when I
first agreed to work with him, Matthew is an extremely
intelligent young man, and like most highly intelligent
people he is instinctively adept at diversion and
obfuscation. Over the course of my more than ten years
in practice, I have, however, encountered a great many
highly intelligent young men and women, and have become
extremely skilled at recognizing when I am being told
what the client believes I want to hear, and when I am
being diverted away from subjects that the client finds
uncomfortable. It goes with the territory, especially in
cases involving trauma, where people are commonly
unwilling to discuss topics that are painful or exposing,
at least to begin with.

304

In this instance, Matthew was unusually forthcoming about his continued nightmares. He was reluctant to get into the specifics, but where he has previously been resistant to even admitting their existence, almost certainly because he equates them with weakness, with some kind of failure on his part, he readily admitted to still suffering from them, and appeared engaged when I talked him through some relaxation exercises that have provided short-term relief in other similar cases.

He was, however, extremely reluctant to discuss the return of Lauren Bailey. He attempted to derail my questions in a number of ways, initiating discussions of the politics of high school and his opinions of Lauren's friends and their mutual classmates. However, two things became clear to me.

Firstly, that the disappearance of Lauren Bailey affected Matthew more profoundly than he has previously been willing to acknowledge. The onset of his nightmares obviously predates her disappearance, so there is no direct connection to be drawn between them, but his current emotional state is unquestionably being affected by it. He made reference to the article in The Reporter, *unprompted by me, and expressed his belief that everybody looks at him differently now, even though Lauren returned safely and there is nothing to suggest the article was anything more than mean-spirited gossip. He became quite agitated while discussing Lauren, which leads me to my second observation.*

On several occasions as he talked about Lauren's return, he made reference to "what I did" or similar. I did not press him on what he was referring to, as I felt it would be counter-productive to interrupt him while he was opening up in a way he has previously refused to, but my concern is that

305

he has created some kind of emotional connection between himself and Lauren's return.

It is most likely merely a symptom of the profound relief he feels now that she is back, which in turn relates to the level of concern he has been feeling during her absence and which he has kept almost entirely internalized. And which may well have been exacerbated by The Reporter's *article, which was both unfair and entirely beyond his control.*

I will raise this with Matthew during our next session. I don't believe this is anything to be concerned about at this point – it may, in fact, actually represent a breakthrough in our relationship – but my recommendation would be that we increase our sessions to twice a week.

As always, I am available to discuss this with you both if that will be helpful.

Yours sincerely,

Jennifer Casemiro, M.D.

April 2nd

Journal entry 34

I hid the letter in my room. There's a box of old comics under my bed and I buried it in the middle of them. There's no reason why Mom or Dad would think there was something to look for, but even if they did, they wouldn't find it there.

Reading her letter was painful, like everything I thought I had put up as defenses around me were just windows that she could see straight through.

I don't remember being "agitated." My memory of the session is that I was calm. I *felt* calm, like I was in control, like I could anticipate what she was going to say before she said it, like I could see every trap and sudden curve coming, like it was all easy.

I don't remember mentioning what I did.

I don't remember that at all.

Fuck.

— — — —

TRANSCRIPTS OF AUDIO RECORDED ON MATTHEW BARKER'S CELLPHONE

Recording begins: April 3, 03:21

I should just set my alarm for 3.14 every morning now. It would be easier.

The dreams aren't going to stop. I feel like I know that now, like someone has turned a switch on inside my head and everything is suddenly clear. I thought they were about Lauren, about what I saw in her photos, and maybe they still are, at least a little. But they've moved past that now. Whatever this is, it's about me.

It's about what I did. What I took from him.

I was lying on my bed and everything looked normal, but I knew I wasn't awake. There was something flickering in the back of my brain, like this sort of softness, a space where something could get in, and I knew I was still dreaming. I think I tried to wake myself up, but nothing happened. And I was just lying there in the dark, staring up at the ceiling, and when the shadows on the wall of my bedroom started to move, I didn't even feel scared.

I felt relieved. Jesus. I know that sounds crazy, but it's the truth. Because when they moved, I knew what this was. And it didn't even feel bad. I don't know how else to say it.

It didn't feel bad.

The shadows ran together on the ceiling above me, and I couldn't look away and I couldn't move. I couldn't even close my eyes. I had to watch as they rolled and stretched and came together until he was there, and he was looking down at me with that face with no features, with no eyes. That white space that looks like nothing but is everything. The black tentacles and the long limbs and the angles that make it look like he's wearing a suit, that I can totally see why that's how people shopped him to look, but he isn't. There aren't any clothes there at all, no shirt and no tie and no jacket. There's just him, the shape of him. The blackness that moves. The shadows that have become solid.

Fuck.

There's no eyes and there's no mouth and there's nothing at all, just space and black and white, but I knew he was looking at me and I knew he was smiling down at me, and it might just have been because I couldn't move and he knew I was trapped but that wasn't how it felt. It felt like he was smiling at me because he wanted me to know something, to understand something.

It felt like he was encouraging me. Like he wanted me to do something, but he didn't want to have to make me do it. Like he wanted me to do it myself. And I stared at him and he stared down at me as the shadows snaked and twisted and I felt something come loose inside my head and I understood.

And the tentacles turned and they started to move down from the ceiling, and then I think I screamed because I stared into that white emptiness where his face should be and there was no smile anymore, there was nothing but freezing cold, the temperature of death, and I screamed as the tentacles got closer because the only thing that I could think, the one thought that was crunching through my head, was that I couldn't let them touch me. I just could not allow that to happen.

And then I woke up.

I don't think I screamed out loud. Or if I did, I don't think anyone heard. I waited a couple of minutes before I recorded this, but there's no sound in the apartment.

Jesus. Honestly.

I think.

No. I don't think. I know.

I know what I have to do. I think I've always known, deep down. And I understood the threat. I know what the price will be if I don't, if I'm not brave enough to see this through.

I know.

Recording ends: April 3, 03:25

April 3rd

When I got home from school, my laptop screen was glowing on my desk.

I turned it off before I went to school this morning.

I really clearly remember doing so, because I normally don't. Normally I just close it. But it's been running slowly and sometimes shutting it down properly and leaving it off for a few hours does the trick. So I remember emptying the trash and I remember closing all the applications and I remember shutting it down. I remember hearing the fan stop spinning.

And now it's on. And there's a file in the middle of my desktop that wasn't there this morning. That hasn't ever been there, even though the information claims it was created two years ago, by me.

The file is called coda.docx.

And I didn't create it. I've never seen it before. And I don't want to open it, but I know I'm going to, because how can I not? We're past the point where any of this is optional, where I could just call timeout and say I'm not playing anymore.

That isn't how this works.

— — — —

CODA

A month after Mary Cooper came home, the men and women of the village held Stephen's funeral, even though there was no body to bury.

The forest had been searched thoroughly by the King's Master at Arms and three garrisons of the Castle Guard, but no sign had been found of him. Because of his position as the Lord of Wrong Side, there had only been a certain amount of time that could be allowed to elapse before matters had to be taken in hand. A new Lord was needed, and that meant officially listing the previous one as dead.

Some of the villagers had protested, but there had been little they could say. Stephen had gone searching for Mary Cooper and had not returned, and it was just as simple as that. He had taken no horse, no provisions beyond the basic. Even if – as some still liked to claim – he had grown weary of his responsibilities and used Mary's disappearance as an elaborate way for him to disappear into the night without arousing suspicion, he was presumably never coming back. So what needed to be done was done, with a stroke of the King's quill.

The new Lord was a cousin of the King, who had never set foot in Wrong Side in his life. He was refusing to live in his new territory until suitably grand accommodation could be built for him, and was staying in apartments in the castle while the work was carried out. He had visited the village twice, and the look on his face, similar to that of a man who has trodden in shit and is just now starting to smell it, had reminded those of sufficient years of Alice Webster.

Mary Cooper spoke at Stephen's funeral, although there was little she could say apart from express her gratitude. She had no memory of the time between when she went to bed after returning from her walk with Arthur Allen and when she woke up near the edge of the forest, shivering and covered in morning dew. She had tried to remember more, if for no other reason than to satisfy the endless questions about where she had been and what had happened to Stephen, but there was nothing there. It was as though there was a black hole in the center of her mind, one that she already suspected was unlikely to ever be filled.

They sang songs as an empty coffin was lowered into the ground, and they drank ale in the yard of the Cooper farm and told tales of the man they had said farewell to. Men who had served under him in the Borderlands spoke of his heroism, of his bravery and good character. Sarah Cooper simply thanked him for bringing her daughter home, and raised her mug to the heavens.

The following summer, Mary Cooper and Arthur Allen were married. Barely three months later – to the scandalous delight of the villagers – she gave birth to a son.

At his mother's insistence, the boy was named Stephen.

April 3rd

Journal entry 36

OK.

Message received.

I get it.

— — — —

Breaker1989 <breakerbreaker1989 @gmail.com>

To: RightHereRightThere <righthere8rightthere9@gmail.com>

Date: 3 April at 16:39

Subject: I know what I have to do

I think I've always known, deep down. But it's clear now. It's really clear.

I have to go back into the darkness, and I have to confront him. If I don't, then when he's done with me he'll go back to Lauren. And I can't let that happen.

It's the only way for this to be over.

I get it now.

RightHereRightThere <righthere8rightthere9@gmail.com>

To: Breaker1989 <breakerbreaker1989 @gmail.com>

Date: 3 April at 16:52

Subject: RE: I know what I have to do

I would love to tell you not to do this, that we'll think of something else, that there's another way. But I think we both know there isn't.

You're a fucking hero, Matt. I'm proud to know you, even just a little. And I'm not going to say goodbye, because fuck that.

Instead, I'll just say Godspeed. And, as always, be careful.

Ryan

April 3rd
Journal entry 37

I managed to not laugh out loud when he suggested I be careful.
That doesn't really feel like a possibility anymore, but it's OK. I just
needed to tell someone, so that at least someone knows that I've
made a decision, that I know what I need to do and I'm going to
do it.

I have to finish this myself.

— — — —

TRANSCRIPTS OF AUDIO RECORDED ON PAUL BARKER'S CELLPHONE

Recording begins: April 3, 20:31

MATTHEW BARKER: That was great, Mom. Thanks.

KIMBERLEY BARKER: You're welcome. Nice to have you out here with us instead of in your room.

MATTHEW BARKER: Like you said the other day, we should do this more often.

KIMBERLEY BARKER: I'd really like that.

PAUL BARKER: Me too.

KIMBERLEY BARKER: How was school today?

MATTHEW BARKER: It was OK.

KIMBERLEY BARKER: How's Lauren handling being back?

MATTHEW BARKER: I don't know. Fine?

KIMBERLEY BARKER: It seemed early to go back to school, to me. Didn't you think so?

PAUL BARKER: I did.

MATTHEW BARKER: I guess she felt ready? She probably wanted things to go back to normal.

KIMBERLEY BARKER: I think that's what everyone wants.

MATTHEW BARKER: Right.

PAUL BARKER: I can't stop wondering where she was.

KIMBERLEY BARKER: Paul.

PAUL BARKER: I know, right. No good in speculating. I get that. It's just ...

KIMBERLEY BARKER: She's back. That's all that matters.

PAUL BARKER: Yeah. Yeah.

MATTHEW BARKER: How are her parents doing?

KIMBERLEY BARKER: They're OK, I think.

MATTHEW BARKER: There was stuff in the paper. About her dad moving out.

PAUL BARKER: You should really know not to believe what you read in the tabloids.

MATTHEW BARKER: So they're good?

KIMBERLEY BARKER: They're working things out. Right now, they're just focused on Lauren.

MATTHEW BARKER: OK.

PAUL BARKER: What about you, Son?

MATTHEW BARKER: What about me?

KIMBERLEY BARKER: Are you really OK? I know it must have been hard while she was missing.

MATTHEW BARKER: It was. But it's OK. I'm just relieved she's back.

PAUL BARKER: Ditto.

KIMBERLEY BARKER: I'm still so angry about that article.

MATTHEW BARKER: I know. Me too. But we can't do anything about it now.

PAUL BARKER: Nope. What's done is done.

MATTHEW BARKER: Right.

KIMBERLEY BARKER: And anyone who can't see that you were having a hard time with Lauren missing is just trying to see bad where there isn't any.

PAUL BARKER: Yep. Fuck those people.

KIMBERLEY BARKER: Paul!

MATTHEW BARKER: Thanks, Dad.

PAUL BARKER: You're welcome, Son.

KIMBERLEY BARKER: We love you, Matt. And we're very proud of you.

MATTHEW BARKER: I love you guys too.

Recording ends: April 3, 20:36

April 3rd

Journal entry 38

I think that went OK.

I think it did.

And it doesn't really matter. Not anymore.

I'm not going to leave them anything. You write notes for the people you love when you know you're not coming back, and **this is not what this is.**

I know where I'm going and I know what I have to do but I'm coming back.

I confronted him once already and Lauren came back and I came back and that's what's going to happen this time too.

So I'm not leaving anything for Mom and Dad. Because this isn't some bullshit sacrifice. This isn't giving up. This is walking into the darkness and doing what has to be done because it's the right thing to do.

I'm not leaving them anything.

I'm not.

— — — —

APRIL 22ND 2018, 20TH POLICE PRECINCT STATION-HOUSE, MANHATTAN, NY

Participants:
Detective John Staglione
Detective Mia Ramirez
Jamie Reynolds
Donald McArthur (Attorney-at-Law)

DET. STAGLIONE.   What happened that morning?

JAMIE REYNOLDS.   When Matt disappeared?

DET. RAMIREZ.   Right.

JAMIE REYNOLDS.   Everything started all over again. The assemblies, the emails to parents. The school went back into crisis mode.

DET. RAMIREZ.   How did people react?

JAMIE REYNOLDS.   Most people were worried about him. A lot of people blamed Steve. He caught a lot of shit.

DET. STAGLIONE.   Why?

JAMIE REYNOLDS.   It wasn't like with Lauren, where everyone thought she would come back. People thought the worst straight away. Because of everything that had happened, the article in *The Reporter* and all that stuff that got posted online after.

DET. RAMIREZ.   People thought he might have hurt himself?

JAMIE REYNOLDS.   Some people. Yeah.

DET. RAMIREZ.   What about Lauren?

JAMIE REYNOLDS.   What about her?

DET. STAGLIONE.   What did she think had happened?

JAMIE REYNOLDS.   I don't know. I heard from somebody that it really messed her up, and I know she didn't come back to school for about a week. But I never talked to her about it.

DET. RAMIREZ.   Why not?

JAMIE REYNOLDS.   We're not that close.

DET. STAGLIONE.   Did you try to do anything? When Matt disappeared?

JAMIE REYNOLDS.   I texted him. Called him.

DET. RAMIREZ.   Did you get any response?

JAMIE REYNOLDS.   You know I didn't. You found his phone in the park.

DET. STAGLIONE.   The SIM card was missing. Does that seem weird to you?

JAMIE REYNOLDS.   I don't know. Maybe he had another handset?

DET. STAGLIONE.   Maybe. Did you talk to his parents?

JAMIE REYNOLDS.   Yeah. There was a thing at their apartment, after he'd been gone a week. They invited me.

DET. STAGLIONE.   A thing?

JAMIE REYNOLDS.   After they found his journals.

DET. RAMIREZ.   OK.

JAMIE REYNOLDS.   I think they knew then. That he wasn't coming back. So I think they wanted to see if anyone knew anything they didn't. I think they were trying to put it all together.

DET. RAMIREZ.   Do you think it helped?

JAMIE REYNOLDS.   I have no idea. His mom cried the whole time we were there.

DET. STAGLIONE.   Have you read the journals?

JAMIE REYNOLDS.   Of course not. They weren't giving out copies.

DET. RAMIREZ.   Would you like to?

JAMIE REYNOLDS.   What would be the point of that?

DET. STAGLIONE.   What do you mean?

JAMIE REYNOLDS.   I mean, what would be the point? His parents have read them, and I know you've read them, so what would I add to that? And to be honest, I don't want to know what he was going through those last couple of weeks. I'd rather remember him like he was.

DET. STAGLIONE.   So you don't think he's coming back?

JAMIE REYNOLDS.   I didn't say that.

DET. RAMIREZ.   You're talking about how you want to remember him. That doesn't sound like you think you're going to see him again.

JAMIE REYNOLDS.   I hope I do.

DET. RAMIREZ.   Do you think he's still alive?

JAMIE REYNOLDS.   I think I'd like to stop now.

*   *   *   *

Amy Linares

Does Matt Barker live on West 87th?   07:42

José Sanchez

I think so?   07:44

Jamie Reynolds

Yeah. Why?   07:45

Amy Linares

Which building?   07:45

Jamie Reynolds

The Dorset.   07:46

Amy Linares

Shit.   07:46

Andy Lindburgh

What?   07:46

Amy Linares

I just walked past there. There are cops
outside it.   07:47

Jamie Reynolds

Cops?   07:47

Amy Linares

Lots of them.   07:48

Send message

TRANSCRIPTS OF AUDIO RECORDED ON MATTHEW BARKER'S CELLPHONE

Recording begins: April 4, 03:09

It's dark out here. But it feels different.

I can see my breath in front of my face even though I'm wearing a coat and I put a thick sweater on before I sneaked out of the apartment. It's noisy on Central Park West, like it always is I guess, and the park is dark in front of me and the fence looks tall like it did last time but I'm walking toward it and it feels different.

Last time I was scared. I didn't know what was waiting for me.

But I do now. And I'm not scared this time. I feel OK, weirdly.

I feel OK.

Recording ends: April 4, 03:10

Recording begins: April 4, 03:14

I made it over the fence no problem. Didn't catch myself on it, didn't stumble. I just glided up and over, like it wasn't barely there. It felt easy. Maybe it is. Maybe something's making it easy for me. Clearing the path.

The lights are still on in the park and I can hear voices from people who aren't supposed to be in here but they know the rangers are only going to chase them so far. If I was homeless, I'd probably sleep in here. There's got to be less chance of getting rolled or getting raped in here than out on the streets. Unless you climb over the wrong wall and get eaten by the polar bear, I reckon it's got to be pretty safe.

Not for me. But for other people.

I'm going to get off the path now. I'm heading north, toward the reservoir, and I don't know if there's something I'm supposed to do to make it be like last time, like it was when I went for Lauren, but I think I'm somewhere close to where I went into the trees then so I'm going to do it again. Maybe it doesn't matter. I'm sure he knows I'm here.

That I'm coming.

Recording ends: April 4, 03:16

Recording begins: April 4, 03:21

It's dark now. I'm in the trees, but it's not that. The lights have gone out.

I can sort of remember how I felt last time, and it feels weird. It feels like I wasn't thinking at all, like all that was in my head was getting Lauren back and nothing else mattered, there wasn't any room for anything else. This time I feel calm. I feel like I'm in control. My heart is barely even beating fast.

There's darkness all around me and I can hear the sound of birds, can hear the flapping of their wings, and it sounds like there are thousands of them, but I'm not scared.

There's something moving around beside me, something that writhes and glides and twists and comes so close that I could touch it, but I'm not scared.

There's a light ahead of me and it isn't the blue light that was Lauren, it's a black light, like the absence of light, like the end of everything, but I'm not scared.

I'm going to walk toward it.

Recording ends: April 4, 03:23

Recording begins: April 4, 03:24

There's light everywhere. It's black and it shines and it moves like oil and I'm somewhere else now, somewhere cold and dark and I'm not alone. There's something here with me. The light is part of it, or it's part of the light, I don't know, oh God, I don't know and I don't want to be here anymore, I don't want this, I don't fucking want this.

It's moving.

I can see.

Oh God, I can finally see.

I can

Recording ends: April 4, 03:25

Storytime. (i.redd.it)(Slender_Man)

submitted 2 hours ago * by righthererightthere

So I've been helping a guy who sometimes posts on this board write a Slender Man story. I'm not going to pretend it's real, or get all spooky, because it doesn't need that. It's just a really great, really clever story that mixes in some weird real-life stuff that I think people on this sub will really enjoy.

Some of it was already posted here, but I've compiled everything into a Dropbox folder. I've numbered all the files in the order you need to open them, because there are audio files as well as text documents and screengrabs from this sub.

If you like it – and I'm really confident you will – you need to direct your praise (and gold!) to u/breakerbreaker1989 – it was his idea, and he did the vast majority of the work. I just played along when he needed me to, and maybe helped guide the story a little here and there. He hasn't posted for a while – I'm sure he's working on some new awesome thing – but I'm sure he'll be glad to hear if you enjoyed it…

Here's the link – dropbox.com/jhgeem02

Enjoy!
8 comments share save hide give gold report

all 28 comments
sorted by **oldest**

[-] jkkhh 0 points 2 hours ago
Wow. This must have taken ages to plan. Seriously great stuff.
perma-link embed save report give gold reply

[-] armystrong45 0 points 2 hours ago
This is genius. Someone give u/breakerbreaker1989 a book deal ASAP. Sort of messed up to use a real missing girl, but that just made it creepier.
perma-link embed save report give gold reply

[-] **jkkkhh** 0 points 2 hours ago

So clever. I just Googled her and she's back now anyway?

perma-link embed save report give gold reply

> [-] **armystrong45** 0 points 2 hours ago
>
> Yeah, I saw that too.
>
> perma-link embed save report give gold reply

[-] **vic32shaker** 1 points 2 hours ago

Solid creepypasta. Don't think I'd be happy if I was that girl's parents.

perma-link embed save report give gold reply

[-] **warl0ck_mndfck** 0 points 2 hours ago

The audio was cool. He's not the greatest actor, but he managed to sound pretty scared when he was describing the dreams.

perma-link embed save report give gold reply

> [-] **jkkkhh** 0 points 1 hour ago
>
> He might just have written them and got someone else to record them.
>
> perma-link embed save report give gold reply

> > [-]**warl0ck_mndfck** 0 points 47 minutes ago
> >
> > Yeah, maybe.
> >
> > perma-link embed save report give gold reply

[-] **6darwin$** 0 points 1 hour ago

I saw the first two parts when he posted them. Knew it was going to be good.

perma-link embed save report give gold reply

[-] **jacktorrancesAAbutton** 0 points 1 hour ago

I guess I'm not seeing it. It's pretty derivative, and some of it's really badly written.

perma-link embed save report give gold reply

> [-] **jkkkhh** 0 points 54 minutes ago
>
> Disagree.
>
> perma-link embed save report give gold reply

> > [-] **jacktorrancesAAbutton** 0 points 50 minutes ago

Wow. You really convinced me. Bravo.
perma-link embed save report give gold reply

[-] **cr€€pypa$ta** 0 points 1 hour ago
Some of the allegory fantasy story was posted in r/creativewriting
a couple of years ago. He's either been planning this a long time or
he found a really cool way to reuse an old story.
perma-link embed save report give gold reply

> [-] **jkkkhh** 0 points 1 hour ago
> I liked those sections. I got straight away that they were go-
> ing to mirror what 'really' happened, but I thought they were
> cool. He writes different styles really well.
> **perma-link embed save report give gold reply**

> > [-] **cr€€pypa$ta** 0 points 1 hour ago
> > I could have done without them TBH. But they weren't
> > bad. I just wanted more SM.
> > **perma-link embed save report give gold reply**

> > > [-] **jkkkhh** 0 points 1 hour ago
> > > See, I liked the fact that SM is used sparingly.
> > > The best SM stories are always about his effect
> > > on normal people, rather than actually about him.
> > > **perma-link embed save report give gold reply**

> > > > [-] **armystrong45** 0 points 32 minutes ago
> > > > This.
> > > > **perma-link embed save report give gold reply**

[-] **liberalismisamentalillness** 0 points 1 hour ago
Not cool. I hope that girl's parents sue the shit out of you.
perma-link embed save report give gold reply

> [-] **staxnstax** 0 points 22 minutes ago
> Triggered much?
> **perma-link embed save report give gold reply**

> > [-] **liberalismisamentalillness** 0 points 18 minutes ago
> > Eat a dick.
> > **perma-link embed save report give gold reply**

[-] **staxnstax** 0 points 16 minutes ago
Homophobic much?
perma-link embed save report give gold reply

[-] **jcvd000** 0 points 1 hour ago
The people who replied to his posts like this shit was all real are
going to be disappointed this morning J
perma-link embed save report give gold reply

> [-] **dinamomk** 0 points 1 hour ago
> Nah. They were just playing along.
> perma-link embed save report give gold reply

>> [-] **jcvd000** 0 points 1 hour ago
>> WAIT. Are you telling me SM isn't real??? J
>> perma-link embed save report give gold reply

>>> [-] **dinamomk** 0 points 58 minutes ago
>>> Shit. I've got to break something about Christmas
>>> to you.
>>> perma-link embed save report give gold reply

[-] **dodgers_suck** 0 points 49 minutes ago
That audio of him going to rescue the girl in Central Park scared
the crap out of me.
perma-link embed save report give gold reply

> [-] **0traveler0** 0 points 34 minutes ago
> Me too. Good stuff.
> perma-link embed save report give gold reply

[-] **KJ_Parker_is_God** 0 points 12 minutes ago
6.5/10
perma-link embed save report give gold reply

October 5 2018. NEW YORK.

BENEFIT HELD ON SIX-MONTH ANNIVERSARY OF TEEN'S DISAPPEARANCE

by Nicole Sheridan

The parents of teenager Matthew Barker, who went missing from the family's Upper East Side apartment one year ago yesterday, last night threw a glittering gala in the ballroom of the Plaza Hotel which raised more than a million dollars for mental health charities in the New York area.

The event was hosted by Paul and Kimberley Barker, who both spoke at length about the year-long ordeal they have endured since their son left their apartment in the middle of the night, and has not been seen or heard from since. Matthew Barker's cellphone was found in Central Park during widespread searches in the subsequent days, although its missing SIM card has led some to speculate that the Riley School senior had planned his disappearance.

Matthew had been rumored to have been involved with the disappearance of his classmate Lauren Bailey, as reported at the time in this column, although no evidence was subsequently found to back up that assertion.

Lauren Bailey and her parents were in attendance last night, although all refused to comment when contacted afterwards. Dr. Lawrence Bailey, whose OBGYN clinic on Madison Avenue counts a number of A-listers among its clients, was briefly estranged from his wife during their daughter's disappearance, amid widespread rumors of infidelity.

No press were allowed to attend last night's gala, although sources have informed this reporter that the guests included many well-known members of the elite New York social scene. I have it on good authority that there were no less than three Tony Award Winners in attendance, along with a large number of Wall Street CEOs and COOs.

An NYPD spokesman confirmed that although Matthew Barker's missing person case remains open, there have been no recent developments of note.

LAUREN

Matt?

LAUREN

Are you there?

LAUREN

It's OK. Just let me know.

LAUREN

I dreamed about you again.

LAUREN

Matt?

LAUREN

Matt?

 Message   Send